THE LONG NIGHT

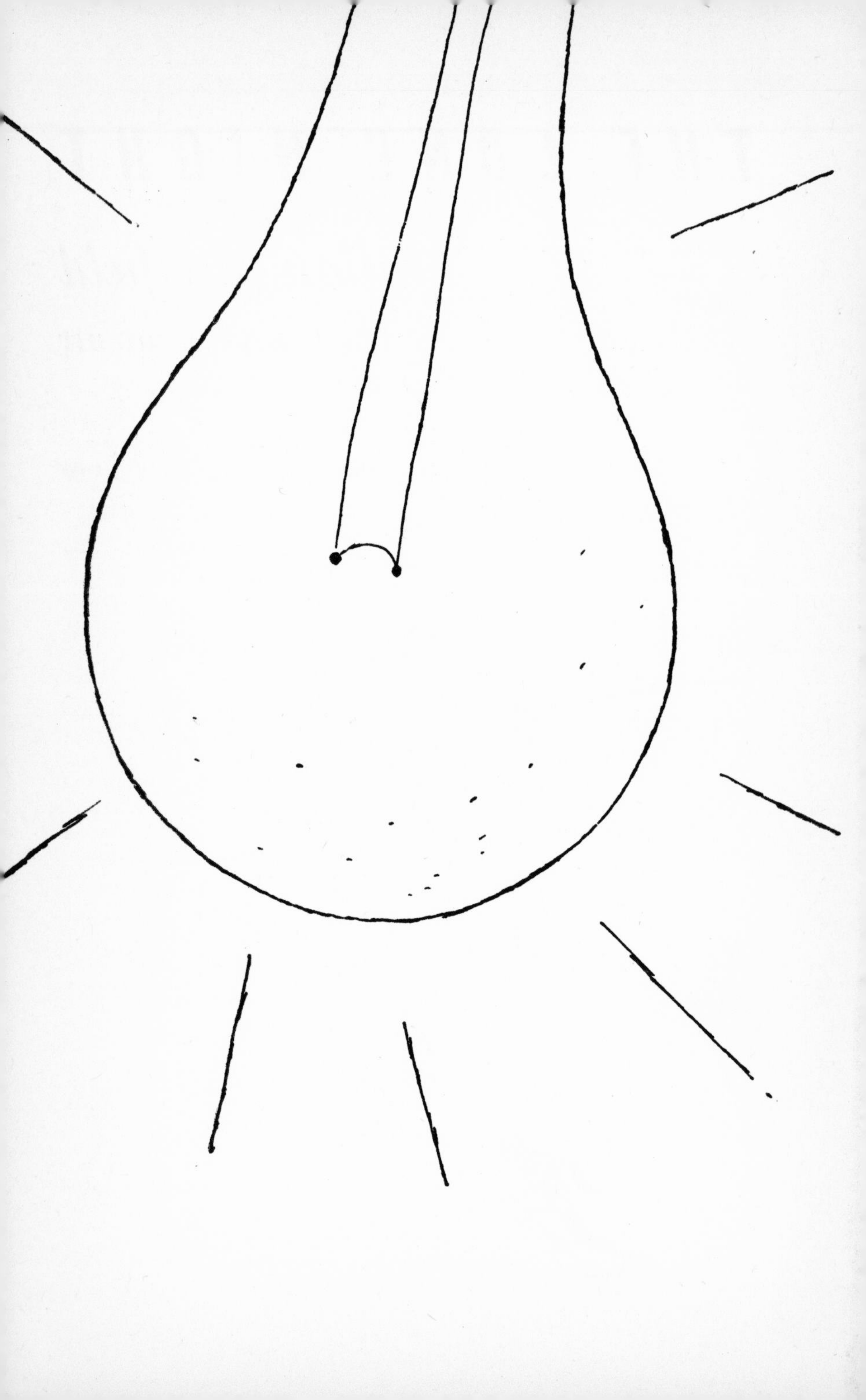

THE LONG NIGHT

Julian Mayfield

author of THE HIT

THE VANGUARD PRESS, INC. NEW YORK

Published simultaneously in Canada by the
Copp Clark Publishing Company, Ltd., Toronto

Library of Congress Catalogue Card Number: 58-12188
Designed by Marshall Lee
Manufactured in the United States of America by
H. Wolff, New York, N.Y.

Quotation on quotation page,
and pages 28, 107, and 123 from
The Divine Horsemen, *by Maya Deren.*

Agwé Arroyo, protect your children,

Sea-shell in hand, care for your little ones . . .

A Voudoun prayer to the Haitian sea god Agwé.

TO ANA LIVIA

THE LONG NIGHT

one

The hallway was dark because the light bulb had burned out a long time ago. Probably one or another of the tenants had thought of replacing the bulb from time to time, but no one had ever got around to doing it. Neither had the old, alcoholic superintendent, who, as much as possible, avoided climbing stairs. So once you reached the fifth floor of this Harlem tenement, you found yourself in almost complete blackness. But the enveloping sounds and smells told you that you were still among the living. Radios and television sets squawked, and people hollered at one another behind invisible doors. A heavy staleness hung in the hallway, relieved only by the occasional piquancy of hotly seasoned frying pork. You saw, after your eyes became adjusted, that there was a vague light after all. Along the dank hallway you could now discern several heavy wooden doors, some with ancient, grease-filled cracks in them. The doors stood in a line like weary old soldiers in the night, protecting the living quarters beyond.

At the rear of this hallway was an apartment of two small rooms. Here on a warm Saturday afternoon Lieutenant Frederick Brown, ten years old, lay on his cot reading a Superman comic. He was waiting for his mother to come home from the laundry where she worked. She would relieve him of the guard duty he was standing over his little brother and baby sister.

He was a member-in-good-standing of The Comanche Raiders, the dominant neighborhood club. All the boys now called him Steely because he had gone through the initiation exercises without a whimper. Just before he had run the gantlet, made up of the biggest boys in the club, he had told himself that he wouldn't cry, that he mustn't cry. Some of the blows had been sharp, but he had gritted his teeth and run on. One of the boys had suddenly stuck out his leg and tripped him, spilling him to the ground with tremendous impact, scratching his arms and face and causing his nose to bleed. But he had not cried out or even opened his mouth. He had crawled until he could struggle to his feet. Then he had run on, ignoring the grinning faces and the yelled threats and the strange cruel looks in the faces of the boys about to strike him. He had run on, knowing that he had already been through the worst and that he would pass the test all right. At the end of the ceremony the Supreme Commander, Shotgun (the one who had tripped him), nicknamed him Steely and commissioned him a Second Lieutenant in The Junior Comanche Raiders, which was the section of the club that a boy served in until he was thirteen. Steely was very proud of his rank because the other boys who had undergone the same initiation were only sergeants. None of the boys his own age ever challenged him any more. Even those guys two years older knew that Steely was nobody's push-over.

He was a very black boy, tall for ten years old, but skinny. He knew better than to wrestle when he got into a fight because the average boy had the advantage of weight and could slam him to the ground. But Steely was fast and slippery. He could hit and move away and hit again before his opponent knew what was happening.

And he could run. Nobody could run like Steely. When the cops came on the scene Steely took off like a bat out of hell, and even the older boys had a hard time catching up. Running was his passion. When he felt confused and angry and did not know what to do about it, he would take off, his black knees pumping up and down, his sneakers hardly seeming to touch the sidewalk. Sometimes Steely would run for no reason at all, just because he had nothing else to do. Off he would go with no particular place in mind, running until he was exhausted. Then he would slow down to a walk. All his strength would be gone, but he would feel better somehow, freer.

Suddenly he sat up on the cot and yelled, "Get out of that window!"

His five-year-old brother, Robby, a bumptious, obstinate boy, liked to play in the window leading to the fire escape. Steely knew that a lieutenant's principal duty was to maintain discipline; his voice was sharp and hard when he spoke to Robby. Seeing that Robby was slow about obeying the order, Steely lunged at his brother, caught him by the waist of his short pants, and jerked him back into the room. Such arbitrary treatment infuriated the younger boy. He swung wildly but missed. Contemptuously Steely pushed him to the floor, where he sat with his legs outstretched. He opened his mouth and let out a howl. This woke Carol Ann, who was only a little over a year old. She sat up in her crib and gave a long frightened wail. The children's crying sounded like a duet of sick air-raid sirens.

"Shut up!" Steely screamed at them, but they only yelled louder. He decided to ignore Robby. He went to the crib, which they had bought second-hand at the Salvation Army and painted a bright yellow. He took his sister in his arms and hugged her. She was only a baby, Steely reminded himself, and he could understand why she might not show proper respect for his authority. He loved Carol Ann and told her so now as he rocked her back and forth, kissing her cheeks and her little arms and hands. She stopped crying and laughed and started to play with his ears. Robby's interest was attracted by two fuzzy blue-black flies that flew through the open window and hovered over the pots on the stove. He stopped crying and rolled up an old magazine. There was nothing he hated more than flies. He took vicious but ineffectual whacks at them, exhaling anguished grunts as he saw how little damage he was doing. After setting Carol Ann back into her crib, Steely went to his cot and opened his comic book again.

Being a leader was very important to Steely. His father had told him about Toussaint L'Ouverture, a black Haitian who had revolted against Napoleon and liberated his people from slavery. Steely's father had also told him about the great Douglas, after whom he had been named Frederick—a man who had been born a slave in the United States but had overcome many obstacles and become a great leader of his people. That was the kind of goal Steely was determined to reach. To attain it he would be hard and unafraid and would risk death a thousand times.

But neither Toussaint nor Frederick Douglas were as real to him as his other heroes, Superman and Davy Crockett. True, it made a great difference that Toussaint and Frederick Douglas had been colored men, but not everyone had heard of them. Superman and Davy Crockett were famous. If a game was being organized on the street and you said you were either of these two, the other guys did not ask, "Who's that?"

So now as he stretched on his cot he was not Steely any more but Superman, the strongest person in the whole world. He could lift anything, run faster than a bullet, and his eyes were so powerful that he could see through a steel wall. Best of all, he could fly like a jet plane, even faster. When there was a war he could knock them out of the sky with one hand. Now he glided lazily over Harlem, swooping down occasionally and scattering his enemies. At One Hundred and Twenty-third Street, with one great blow he completely demolished The Black Ravens, who were traditionally the bitterest enemies of The Comanche Raiders. Picking up speed, he soared eastward over One Hundred and Eighth Street and Madison Avenue, where the Puerto Rican boys lived. When he found the clubroom of The Conquistadores he brought his fist down hard and The Conquistadores were destroyed forever. Then he sped southward over Yorkville where the white boys were gathered. There he swept all The Avengers and The Hawks into the East River and watched happily as each of them drowned.

Steely sighed. The first thing he would do if he were really Superman would be to circle low over Harlem until he saw his father below. He would swoop down, catch his father in his arms, and soar with him through the clouds high above New York. Steely would tell his father how mad his mother was but that she would probably let him come back home. Then Steely would ask the question that was bothering him, the one that only his father could answer—

Smack!

The blow was a hard, thumping one across the back of his head. It knocked him off the cot onto the floor.

Smack!

This time it exploded on the side of his face, stinging and hurting him, jarring his whole body, making him see bright red and yellow dabs. He huddled against the wall and tried to cover his face with his hands, expecting that another blow was impending. He made a point of never crying, but right now he hurt very much.

"Damn you, Frederick! I thought I told you to watch these kids. I can't trust you to do nothing, can I? Look at that boy up there in that window!"

It was his mother. He parted his fingers and peeped into her face. The familiar deep brown eyes were fastened on him accusingly. Her dark lips were thin and tight. Quickly he shifted his gaze to the window. Again Robby was playing happily on the fire escape. He played like a lamb, with no idea of the shock in store for him; the commotion indoors had been drowned out by the street noises. Mae Brown reached out and caught him by the pants. He struggled until he saw that it was his mother who held him. She jerked him into the room and stood him on the floor in front of her.

"How many times have I told you to stay off that there fire escape?" she demanded. "Tell me, huh? How many times, Robby?"

Robby's lips moved but no sound escaped.

Smack!

Robby tried to twist away, but Mae Brown held him fast.

"Are you gonna mind what I tell you and stay out of that window?"

He nodded his head up and down and tried to speak, but fear choked off the sound.

Smack!

She loosened her grip and Robby sat down

where he had been standing. From deep within him, softly at first, then growing ever louder, came wailing, pitiable sobs. Steely's ears still hummed, but his head had stopped hurting. He wished he could cry like Robby—then surely he would not feel so bruised inside. His mother's voice was so even that it was almost a monotone as she spoke angrily to her sons. The threatening words fell quickly and sharply. They were the harshest of Southern sounds, which are seldom very harsh.

"Neither of you is any good for a damn thing. As hard as I work trying to keep this family together! I've told you over and over again that you're gonna have to learn to take care of yourself, but you won't do it. Both of you act just like babies. You, sitting there with your head in that picture book, the house coulda burnt down and you wouldn'a knowed a damn thing about it. And you, if I *ever* catch you out there on that there fire escape again, I'm gonna whip your behind until it smokes. Hush now, Carol Ann"—here softening her tone and hugging the girl to her—"you know your mama loves her little baby, yes she do." Now she shifted her eyes back to the boy on the floor, whose wailing continued on a maddening and exasperating note. "Robby, you better shut up that yelling 'cause you ain't got half of what you will get if I ever, and I mean if I *ever*, catch you out there again. You're both growing up to be no damn good, just like your daddy. You better learn to mind me like I tell you or I'm gonna beat the living daylights out of both of you. Robby, you got just two seconds to shut up that noise. *Two seconds!*"

Obediently the boy stifled his crying. Mae devoted herself to Carol Ann. Steely remembered how different everything had been when his father was home. Mae and Paul Brown had argued sometimes, but they had also laughed a lot. His mother had been nicer then; she was not always yelling at them and slapping them for the least little thing. There had been lots more to eat, too. Both his mother and his father used to bring home good food when they came in from work. After dinner his father would stretch out on one of the cots or sit at the table and tell stories about great colored men. His father was a wonderful storyteller, and Steely liked to listen to the fascinating tales.

"Make some milk for this baby, Frederick," said his mother without looking at him. She called him "Frederick" only when she was angry with him,

"Fred" at other times. He had told her that everybody now called him Steely, but she insisted on using his old name. He went to the cabinet, consisting of three shelves in a wooden frame. It was hooked to the wall beside the sink. Covered with a flowered yellow cloth, it contained nearly everything they used for eating. He took out one of the brown packages and measured the orange powder carefully into a bottle. He filled the bottle from the running faucet, pushed a nipple onto its neck, and shook it.

"Does it have to be heated, Mama?"

"No, boy. Just give it here."

He went back to his cot and sat staring across the room through the open window. Far away and high up, fluffy gray clouds hung over the city. Through the haze of smoke it seemed he could see a thousand tenement roof tops. He lay back on the cot and stared at the ceiling. Nowadays he was always thinking about how life used to be, and it seemed that he could remember every little thing that had ever happened to him. He could remember back a long time, even before Carol Ann was born. He could close his eyes and see his father's face just as if he had seen it only yesterday. Paul Brown was wine-colored, lighter than Mae. He was a slender, active man who always used his hands when he talked, as if he were drawing pictures in the air. He was never without a joke, a riddle, or a story. Usually it was about Negroes and how they were getting ahead. Sometimes he would get so excited he would stand in the middle of the floor and make frantic gestures like one of those street-corner speakers. He was certainly the most wonderful person Steely had ever known.

"Look here, boy," he would say to Steely. "Do you know how lucky you are?"

Steely would know there was a joke working, but he would not know what to say. Before he could put up his dukes Paul would give him a punch and say, "Don't you know you're about the luckiest kid in the whole world because . . ." And then Steely would know it had all been just an excuse to sing.

"Don't you know, boy,
You got a pretty ma?
Say, don't you know, boy,
You gotta a rich, rich pa?

Mae Brown would say, "I ain't denying I'm good-looking, Paul, but where is your riches?"

Paul would answer, "Don't you know that money

makes you unhappy? It's only because I love my family that I don't bring home more money. Right, Fred?" The boy would nod his head, not really understanding, and Paul would laugh and say, "Oh, boy," in that special way of his. When he said that, Steely didn't know why his heart jumped so. Perhaps it was because his father almost sang the two words, stretching out the "oh" on a real low note, then snapping in the "boy" real short.

A moment later Paul would speak seriously. "It's only a little while longer and then I'll have that diploma. I'll be able to get a decent job and we'll live better. You'll see."

That diploma! Nobody showed any real excitement about it, yet Steely had known they were all waiting for it. His father worked in the shipping room of a dress factory downtown. As far back as Steely could remember, Paul Brown would rush home in the afternoon, eat a hurried dinner, then rush out to catch a train for Brooklyn, where he was going to college. Very early Steely had come to believe—to know—that life would be better for them when Paul finished college and got that diploma.

They had made Steely stay at home with Robby that night of the graduation exercises. When Mae and Paul returned, Steely had asked to see the diploma and was disappointed when they told him it would come in the mail. They had been waiting all this time for something that the postman would bring. It didn't seem right.

Their lives had not changed as they had expected. They had gone on living in the same two rooms and eating much the same kind of food. Steely had expected that they would move to a nicer apartment or maybe even buy a house of their own. But Paul had suddenly decided to become a lawyer, and for that he would have to go to school longer. There had been a big argument about it, with Mae saying that Paul had to remember he didn't live in the world by himself, and after all the years of waiting, it was time he put his education to work and got his family out of the dump they were living in. It was a luxury, she had said, his trying to become a lawyer, with a wife and three children to take care of. Besides—she had thrown this in as the argument became more heated—he had not shown himself to be so smart as he evidently thought he was, having had to make up several credits in the last two years. There were good jobs around for college graduates. Why did he have to subject the family to further hardship by indulging some whim of his? This was the gist of Mae's argument, which she had concluded with a flat question: "Anyhow, what in the world ever put this idea into your head?"

Paul Brown had argued that the race needed lawyers. ("What for?" Mae had retorted. "Far as I can see, they're just looking out for Number One like the whites.") Paul said that only by becoming a lawyer could he realize himself. He assured her that he was smarter than she thought he was and that he would make out all right. The thing wrong with Mae was that she had no vision—she couldn't see beyond her nose. He wanted to become something that his children could be proud of, and she had to understand how important that was. He would not be held back, he shouted. Mae Brown threatened that she would leave him, take the children, and force him to support them. Then Paul revealed that he had already registered and paid his tuition, so that was that. Mae was beaten; their lives went on as before. Steely admired his father. He could see that Paul Brown was a man of his word. He never gave in.

Mae put Carol Ann in her crib and set about making dinner. She said to Steely, "Go down the hall to Miz Anderson and see what the number was."

He put on his Comanche Raider jacket. It was luminous green with black arms. The name of the club, in fancy lettering, was on the back above the emblem. The jackets had cost each boy seven dollars and ninety-eight cents, an amount that had taken Steely ten Saturdays to earn. Now he never left the apartment without the jacket, no matter if the distance was long or short, or the weather hot or cold. It called for stern measures on his mother's part to persuade him to leave it off long enough to have it washed. He had earned every cent of the money it had cost, and had the right to wear his jacket proudly.

The hallway was dank and cool. Somebody was frying chicken; Steely could hear the hot grease popping in the frying pan. At another door he sniffed pungent neck bones and boiling turnip greens touched with a piece of fatback. Corn bread was browning in an oven. The smells filled his nostrils and made him hungry. At the end of the hallway he stopped in front of a door and rapped. There was no response, but when he rapped again the peephole snapped open, shooting a beam of white light across the corridor.

"Who that?"

The woman's voice was aggressive and demanding. At the movies Steely had seen people open their doors without knowing who was on the other side, but he had never seen such a thing in real life. Women were especially cautious in always demanding complete identification.

"It's me, Mrs. Anderson," he said. "Steely from down the hall."

"Who?"

"Steely—Frederick Brown from down the hall."

"Oh."

The door swung open and the pale white light from the naked bulb washed into the hallway. The woman was large and yellow with a fluffy, baglike bosom. Her features were shadowed because the light was behind her.

"What you want, Fred?"

"Mama told me to ask you what the number was."

"Tell her it's three-twenty-one," said Mrs. Anderson and closed the door.

"Three-twenty-one," his mother repeated when he had told her. "Are you joking, boy?"

He shook his head and assured her that those were the figures Mrs. Anderson had told him.

"Three-twenty-one," his mother whispered again. Then she laughed and threw her arms around him. He ducked, thinking at first she was going to strike him, but a moment later he knew he was being embraced.

"Dummy, don't you see? That's my number!" She kissed him, making him feel hot and uncomfortable. "I hit!" Immediately she started figuring. "Now we can get you some shoes for school. And we'll get some for Robby, too, because he'll be starting next month. And there're a couple of things we can get for Carol Ann."

Steely's love for his mother always lay just beneath the surface. Now it stirred and was awakened by her happiness. He knew they did not have much money now that his father was gone, and he sensed that she would be nicer to the children if she did not have so many worries. He felt ashamed of all the spiteful thoughts that recently had begun to pass through his mind about her, especially when she slapped him. Shyly, fumblingly, he returned her embrace.

He asked, "What about you, Mama? Ain't you gonna get nothing new for yourself?"

"Heck, what do I need when I got you and Robby and Carol Ann?" But she winked at him.

"Who knows? Maybe I will get me a pair of stockings or something like that."

She wrote out a note and gave it to him. He knew where Mrs. Morgan lived. He was to go there and give her the note. She would give him twenty-seven dollars and some change. "You put your hand in your pocket," said Mae Brown, "and you hold that money tight, and you better not let go of it until you get back here. You hear me?"

He worked his head up and down with enthusiasm. Now he was Lieutenant Steely Brown being sent on a dangerous mission.

"You be careful now, Fred, and you remember what I told you. Come straight back here and don't you stop for *nothing* or *nobody.*" When he got to the door she added, "And if you lose that money, boy, don't you come back at all."

"I won't lose it, Mama," Steely promised. He had just been knighted by the queen. The government was sending him on a top-secret assignment. His life was at stake, but what did that matter when the fate of a nation depended on him? He ran the length of the hallway and down the wooden steps three at a time.

two

Steely plunged into the brownish gray of One Hundred and Sixteenth Street. It was that time of late afternoon when the crisp white light of day suddenly colors and the night shades come. Steely half ran, half walked through the little knots of men and women who still haggled over prices and weights in the Park Avenue market place. Overhead a twilight train pierced the gathering darkness as it hummed toward One Hundred and

Twenty-fifth Street, the Bronx, and points north. As Steely ran, the smells changed swiftly from crated cabbage and collard greens and damp kale to frying fish and pork chops and *cuchifritos.* Here on One Hundred and Sixteenth Street factory girls and shopgirls and office girls hurried homeward in wedged heels and bargain basement dresses; here hurried also the factory boys, the stock boys, the shopboys, the garage boys, the kitchen boys, and the messenger boys; the handlers, the day laborers, the unskilled helpers; rushing toward pocket-sized apartments with their mustard-colored pay envelopes containing their rewards for services rendered to downtown commerce. It was still early for the petty pimps and the two-fifty whores, but a few of these already loitered on the corners near the saloons like hungry, impatient birds of prey. For all these people—the producers and the parasites, the black, brown, yellow, and white, and all the shades thereof—Saturday night exploded with unrepressed fury, releasing stocked-up passions and recharging dwindling hope and wavering confidence. Saturday night was a Roman candle shot aloft once a week, glowing red-hot momentarily, then, toward morning, disintegrating from acute, sensual exhaustion.

But of course nothing of this sort occurred to Steely, the ten-year-old black boy who at times was Superman or Frederick Douglas, Toussaint L'Ouverture or Davy Crockett, and now again was Lieutenant Brown of the Junior Comanche Raiders, an officer charged with high responsibility. The people who walked One Hundred and Sixteenth Street seemed only quick dark shadows to the running boy. At one corner a cluster of fellow Junior Raiders signaled him. Steely returned the signal but did not stop.

"Who that?"

The woman's voice crackled in the hallway like an old phonograph record. It was thin and fragile, as if the knock on the door had awakened old fears. She was looking through the peephole but could not see anyone. Steely stepped away from the door into her line of vision.

"It's me, Mrs. Morgan. Fred Brown." He wondered how many years it would be before everyone called him by his new name. "Miss Mae's boy," he added.

"Oh," she said.

The peephole snapped shut with a metallic click, and from within the unlocking of the door began.

The heavy steel pole of the police lock was lifted from its place and set to one side. Then there were two snap locks, one at the top and another near the bottom, and, finally, the original lock at the knob. Still the door opened only a few inches because of a chain hooked to the wall. At this point the eye that had looked on Steely from the peephole now examined him through the three-inch space, scanning also the hallway behind him. The owner of the eye removed it from the space, closed the door while she unhooked the chain, then swung the door open, and said, "Come on in here, Fred boy. My lands, you sho has growed!"

It was an old person's apartment, very neat and very ugly, with pictures of dead relatives on the tables and walls. There was also an old tapestry representing a stoical camel and three Arabs praying to the setting sun, and a faded green rotogravure portrait of Franklin D. Roosevelt. The numbers lady was a thin little cheese-colored woman whose left eye twitched like static. Her short gray hair was curled tightly and held in place by a ragged black net. Steely stared in fascination at the bulging blue veins standing out in a crazy pattern on her scrawny neck and bony arms. Even as the woman talked, he could not remove his eyes from them, expecting that at any moment one of them would burst, and wondering if the blood that squirted out would be blue.

She hardly glanced at the note Steely gave her, for in truth she could scarcely read her name, although she was a genius at simple mathematics. With a varicosed hand she reached into her flat bosom and withdrew a greasy roll of money. Hurriedly counting out the bills, she gave them to the boy and sent him on his way, after which she began the relocking of the door.

Now he was Superman again. The twenty-seven dollars in his pocket gave him a feeling of extraordinary power, too great for an average body to contain. But nobody knew he was Superman. Nobody recognized him because he was traveling incognito. Everybody thought he was just Steely Brown from One Hundred and Sixteenth Street, but in reality he had the strength to beat up every one of them, even if they were all to attack him at the same time. Whenever he desired, he could leap into the air and fly to any place in the wide world.

But as he passed Black Papa he quickened his step. The old man had parked his pushcart near the curb and was searching through a trash can.

His black skin shone in the fading light like an ancient piece of sculptured bronze. He had a tangled stubble of steel-gray beard, a few strands of which seemed pasted at the back of his shining bald head. He wore one small golden earring. None of the boys had ever heard him say anything but the unintelligible words which, all day long, he mumbled over and over.

Cina, cina, cina,
Dogwé sang, cina lo-gé

So for sport the boys often ran after him and pelted him with stones, chanting

Black Papa, Black Papa,
Can't talk propuh, can't talk propuh.
Black Papa, Black Papa,
Can't talk propuh, can't talk propuh.

The old man would wave his arms at them and chase them away, but he never said anything. Steely always joined in the fun, but when he was alone he hardly dared look at Black Papa. Steely's father had once told him that many years ago Black Papa had been a Haitian seaman who found himself stranded in New York. Having no way to get back home, he had become sick in the mind and taken to collecting junk so that he would have something to eat. Steely had reasoned that if Black Papa were Haitian, he was one of Toussaint's people. He wondered if the great liberator could have looked like this little old man with the pushcart. He tried to picture Black Papa in stately dignity, his arms folded across his chest, epaulets on his shoulders, commanding an army against Napoleon. He did this frequently, but he could never really imagine Black Papa as Toussaint. He never threw stones at Black Papa any more, but he could not very well refuse to take part in the chanting: the fellows would have razzed him and said he was scared.

He forgot about Black Papa as he walked on. He felt again the power that seemed to flow from the smoothly worn bills in his pocket. How wonderful it would be if, just at that moment, he were to meet his father! Then he would ask the question that was bothering him, and surely Paul Brown would give him a good, satisfying answer. Steely looked at all the men he passed on the street, but none of them was Paul Brown. He stopped in front of the Hollywood Bar & Grill where bright red and blue lights darted around the borders of the large plate glass. The jukebox was turned up to full volume.

My baby can't mambo, mambo, mambo
My baby can't mambo, mambo, mambo
My baby can't mambo, mambo, mambo
Gonna put my baby down . . .

A few men were smoking and drinking at the bar, but Paul Brown was not among them. Steely walked away from the glass, depressed now because the thought came to him that he might never see his father again. For several months he had been on an assignment that no one else knew about. Whenever he had a chance he went out of his neighborhood over to Lenox Avenue or Seventh, turning into all the cross streets, looking into every saloon and shoeshine parlor, scanning every face wherever he found men gathered. One day after school he had searched all the way up Amsterdam Avenue above One Hundred and Twenty-fifth Street. He had come home so late that his mother had whipped him with her belt because he would not tell her what he had been doing.

He remembered the day he had given himself the assignment. It was that time when the two detectives had come to the apartment. They were white men, very large, and Steely thought it strange they should look so much alike with their very light blue eyes and clean-shaven reddish faces without even the smallest mustache. Their hard voices seemed jagged in the little room.

"Well, lady, you took your time about getting in touch with us. It's gonna be harder to find him now."

"I figured he'd come back in a few days when he had time to think about it."

"The two of you had a fight, Mrs. Brown?"

"No, not exactly. But we hadn't been getting along too well."

"You say he hasn't been to his job since he left?"

"No, he hasn't. I checked there and got what pay he had coming to him."

"And these names you left at the station, you're sure these are all his friends that you can think of?"

"Yes, that's right."

"Well, don't you worry. If he's still in New York we'll find this Paul Brown for you."

"I just want him to help support these children. They're his as well as mine."

"Yeah, we understand. We'll get in touch with you if anything turns up."

Right then and there Steely had determined to

find Paul Brown first. The police had no business searching for his father. What crime had Paul Brown committed? Steely knew, of course, that something had gone wrong, but it was a family affair and there had been no need to call in these strangers. So for months now he had worked on this assignment, believing he would be the first to find his father. But neither he nor the police had discovered any trace of Paul Brown. As Steely walked toward home, his hand squeezing the roll of bills in his pocket, it occurred to him that his father might be dead. He had never considered this before, nor did he really believe it now. But it was something to think about. His conception of death was such that he felt no sorrow for his father or himself. But there was regret, for if Paul were dead, Steely would never be able to ask his question and he would never hear the answer.

"Hey, pick up on the kid!"

"Yeah, man! Wahooo! What's shaking, Steely?"

If the boy had not been so occupied with his thoughts he would have seen Shotgun, Crazy Mac, Red Louis, and Tommy Morales before they saw him. And he would have found a way to avoid them, probably by crossing the street and waving to them as if he were in a hurry. Better still, he could have retraced his steps to the corner and circled the block altogether. It was not that he had a dislike for these four boys. Indeed, each of them was a person to be admired. But they were so much bigger than he was, and they had the habit of roughing up the Junior Raiders "to make 'em tough." So Steely always avoided them if he could.

These four boys composed the Supreme Council of The Comanche Raiders. Shotgun was a dark brown boy of sixteen who seemed much older. He was squat and fierce-looking. He had acquired his name a couple of years earlier during a gang war when, according to legend, he had fired two blasts of a shotgun from a roof top into the ranks of the enemy and sent them flying. Two of the victims had spent several days in the hospital, but the cops had never been able to find out who had fired the buckshot. The weapon had remained hidden ever since, but its owner had succeeded in giving the impression that on the slightest provocation he would take it from its hiding place and use it. Crazy Mac was so called because of the peculiar way his eyes focused. He was very clever and had the reputation of being able to talk his way out of anything. Red Louis was a tough yellow boy with short red hair and auburn eyebrows and lashes. Tommy Morales had a Puerto Rican mother, spoke Spanish perfectly, and was one of the reasons for the troubled peace that presently existed between The Comanche Raiders and their East Harlem neighbors, The Conquistadores. These four boys determined policy for the Raiders. They had grown up in the neighborhood and were as much a part of the landscape as the red brick of the buildings and the battered trash cans chained to the fences.

"What's happening, kid?"

"Nothing, Shotgun. Same as ever."

"What's shaking with your Juniors?"

"Everything's great. Just great."

Shotgun took a lazy punch at Steely, who ducked his head.

"Crazy, man," said Shotgun, "crazy! This is a quick little kid here. Real fast."

They were gathered under a street light in the middle of the block. The Supreme Council had been discussing different ways to spend their Saturday night. There were a couple of parties in the neighborhood, but these promised to be dull affairs because they already knew all the girls who would probably attend. There was a party in the Bronx to which they had not been invited and at which their appearance would certainly provoke trouble. They had halfway decided on this latter and more dangerous course when Steely arrived; consequently nobody gave the little boy more than distracted attention. But Steely was thoroughly uncomfortable. He could not help thinking of the money clenched in his right hand and of his mother's admonition not to stop for anything.

"Well, see you later," said Steely.

Shotgun said, "Yeah. Later for you, kid."

Steely felt relief. He started toward home. It was Crazy Mac who called him back.

"Hey, Steely. Wait up a minute."

His first thought was to light out for home as fast as his legs could carry him. But he did not want to arouse suspicion. Besides, he was used to doing what the members of the Supreme Council told him. Steely stopped and turned to face Crazy Mac, who now walked toward him.

"What is it?"

"Where're you rushing to?"

"I'm just going home."

Shotgun called, "Hey, Crazy, come on and leave the kid alone. We ain't got all night."

"I will," said Crazy, "just as soon as I see—" He

reached out quickly and gripped Steely's right arm. "—what he's guarding in his pocket there."

"Aw, come on, Crazy," Steely yelled. "My mother told me—" But already his clenched hand was exposed. Steely squeezed the money with all his strength, but the larger boy pressed a thumb into his wrist and he had to let go. Crazy took the money and counted it.

"I knew he was holding something in that pocket," he said with satisfaction.

Now the entire Council was interested. Steely looked furiously from one to the other as they grouped themselves around him and Crazy.

He appealed to Shotgun. "Make him give it back, Shotgun! Please! That's my mother's. Please, Shotgun!"

The Supreme Commander took the money and counted it quickly. He shot a hard look at Steely. "This kid," he said, feigning anger, "is a rat, a stinker, men! Do you hear me?"

The rest of the Council chorused agreement. They winked at one another as their minds were eagerly attempting to divide four into twenty-seven. They were actually fond of Steely in their own peculiar way.

"Imagine," continued the Supreme Commander,

"this little bastard walking around with a fist full of green and holding out on us. After all we've done for him! A rat this kid is! A real rat!"

They grinned. Steely was terrified. The worst thing in the world was happening.

"*Please,* Shotgun!"

"Beat it, kid," said Shotgun with great dignity. "The Council's gonna borrow this loot to cover Certain Emergency Expenses." These last few words were pronounced with relish and pride, as if Shotgun had invented them right there on the spot.

"But it's not mine!"

"I said beat it."

Steely leapt like greased lightning and almost succeeded in snatching the roll from Shotgun's fingers. But he missed, and a blow from the larger boy sent him sprawling onto the sidewalk. He was more outraged and angry than he had ever been in his whole life. He was so angry he literally could hardly see. Like a flash he was on his feet and punching wildly at the Supreme Commander, who held him off with one hand.

"For Chrissakes," laughed Shotgun, "somebody get this little punk off me, will you?"

Just then one of Steely's blows got through Shotgun's guard and struck him flush on the mouth. The gang leader cursed and gave the boy a vicious slap with the back of his hand. Steely was knocked against a building but in an instant he was back, swinging at everyone he could see. A few grown-ups standing nearby had seen the whole thing. They now moved away cautiously. Steely heard a police whistle. The Council of The Comanche Raiders fled down the street. When the police squad car drew up to the sidewalk Steely was the only one there. Exhausted, he sat on the steps trying not to believe in the reality of what had just happened.

"What's going on here, boy?"

He wanted to blurt out everything that had happened to him. He wanted the policemen to take their guns and kill each one of the boys who had robbed him. But he did not believe the cops were any match for Shotgun and the rest of the Council. Also, he knew he would never get his money back, for if the police were to catch the boys they would probably keep the money for themselves. Besides, you were not supposed to tell a cop anything, under any circumstances.

"Nothing," he answered.

When they found out Steely lived in the next

block, one of them, a young man with blond hair, said, "You better get off the street, you little bastard. Next time I catch you in this block after dark I'm gonna run you in."

So Steely walked toward home. His stomach was in a tight little knot and he felt sick. Bitterly he admitted to himself that he was not either Superman, Davy Crockett, Frederick Douglas, or Toussaint L'Ouverture. He was Steely Brown, a little boy who was pushed around by big people. And it would be a long time before he grew large enough to fight them the way he wanted to.

"And if you lose that money, boy, don't you come back at all."

That was the last thing his mother had said before he left home. When Steely reached the place where he lived he stood on the sidewalk and looked fearfully up at the tired old building with its rust-red front. He took a few steps into the hallway, then changed his mind. He had failed in his mission. There was no telling what his mother would do to him. Twenty-seven dollars was a lot of money.

As he walked away he made a vow. He would get another twenty-seven dollars. Somehow, this very night, he would turn his failure into success.

He would come home, give his mother the money, and she would never know the difference. He felt better now, for he was acting like his heroes. None of them would ever admit defeat.

three

Steely was an extremely serious and sensitive boy, but he was not quick-witted. He never took anything lightly. His was really a one-track mind. He searched beneath the surface of everything, even when there was nothing there. His imagination, unusually lively, supplied what was lacking in reality. Completely without guile, when he was faced with a problem he attacked it in the most obvious way, frontally. His dark face was long and thoughtful and was seldom brightened with a smile. His deep brown eyes, which seemed black under certain lights, were so wide and credulous, and yet so uncompromising, that they were disturbing to adults who had learned the ways of the world.

Now, as he walked under the streetlights of One Hundred and Sixteenth Street, his first thoughts were of Mr. Litchstein, who owned a pharmacy in the neighborhood. Steely often cleaned the stock room and the back yard of the store, for which Mr. Litchstein never paid him less than fifty cents and sometimes as much as a dollar.

Two things guided him toward the pharmacy now. Mr. Litchstein was a nice man, and—this was very important—one of the few people who always remembered to call him by his new name. Also, Mr. Litchstein was the only person Steely knew who owned property and he was therefore, to the boy's mind, rich.

Actually the store did not prosper. Its proprietor ignored all the modern methods for attracting people into his place of business. He never turned a salesman away. He would carry any product so long as it did not cost him cash money. Too much stock was displayed, and the store was badly lighted. The fountain had equipment for serving sandwiches, ice cream, and sodas, but there was usually nothing to be had but coffee, which was Mr. Litchstein's favorite beverage.

He was just over fifty years old. His brownish hair was unruly, and had long ago defeated Mr. Litchstein's half-hearted attempts to groom it. What little was left always stood out from the back of his head as if it were being blown by the wind. His quick little eyes, set in a face with large features, looked out on the world with friendly interest and always contained an invitation to exchange views with him. Mr. Litchstein loved to talk, about politics, morality, finance, juvenile delinquency, anything.

The store was, as usual, empty except for a regular customer: a well-dressed, light-complexioned Negro of about the same age, who often dropped in to argue with the pharmacist.

"Jews, Negroes, white folks, race problem," intoned Mr. Litchstein in this conversation, which had begun several weeks before. "That's all I ever hear you talk about. It's a sickness with you. Don't you know anything else to talk about?"

"What are you getting so excited about?" retorted the man. "We're having a civilized conversation. Let's keep it that way."

Mr. Litchstein said, "I always get excited when I hear dangerous ideas. Listen, my friend, there is only one race—" Here he emphasized each word by slowly and insistently striking his palm on the counter. "—and that is the human race!"

"Nuts!" said the customer. Both he and the pharmacist sipped their coffee.

Mr. Litchstein continued. "It is people like you, with your petty frustrations, your petty ambitions, your imagined wrongs—imagined, mind you—that create so much hatred in the world. Oh, hello, Steely." He smiled abruptly at the boy and just as abruptly scowled again as he turned back to the man. "You are blessed and you don't know it. You live in the most wonderful country in the world and you sneer at it. I am not saying everything here is perfect, but at least we can make progress, not like in some countries I could name. You can't deny that the colored people have come a long way. Look at Dr. Ralph Bunche and Marian Anderson and Joe Louis. It's people like that who prove my point."

The man tilted his cup and drained it. "Balls!" he snorted.

Mr. Litchstein flushed red. "Do you know somebody else who was always stirring up race issues?

He was just like you. His name was Adolf Hitler."

The man's coffee went down the wrong pipe and he almost choked. After a spasm of coughing he began to laugh heartily. Mr. Litchstein angrily walked away to the end of the counter, where Steely was standing.

"Do you want something, Steely?"

He smiled and the boy felt reassured, for Mr. Litchstein's smile was as warm as his frown was forbidding. "Yessir," said Steely, "I've got a proposition."

The laughter of the man at the counter still rang inside the store. The pharmacist called to him: "If you find that funny, my friend, you have a very distorted sense of humor." Then he turned back to the boy again. "So you have a proposition, Steely. So let's hear."

"It's like this, Mr. Litchstein . . ." Steely went on to explain that he would clean out the stock room and the back yard of the drugstore and do anything else that needed doing for the next twenty-seven weeks if Mr. Litchstein would advance him the money he needed so badly. The pharmacist was thinking of the next barb he would fire at his laughing adversary. He listened to Steely sympathetically, giving occasional affirmative grunts and nods of his head, but the truth is that he listened with only half an ear. When Steely stopped talking, Mr. Litchstein asked, "And just how much is it you want, Steely?"

The boy eagerly restated the figure. "Twenty-seven dollars."

"Ikes!" cried Mr. Litchstein. The very syllables made him wince as if Steely had pushed a sharp knife between his ribs. Now he gave the boy his full attention, seeing him for the first time.

"Are you serious?"

Steely wagged his head. Mr. Litchstein started to say something but changed his mind. He started to say several things but never got beyond the first word. Finally he sighed and asked, "How old are you, Steely?"

"Ten. I'll be eleven my next birthday."

"Naturally if you're ten you'll be eleven your next birthday," said Mr. Litchstein impatiently. "Steely, don't you know that you should not come to a man who is feeling happy and make him unhappy by asking him for money?"

Steely started to protest. "But I'm gonna—"

Mr. Litchstein held up his hand. "Let me talk, now that you have stated your proposition." Never before had he noticed the boy's eyes. In the black face they seemed almost stark. They accused, they judged, they passed sentence. They were very unfair. Mr. Litchstein swallowed and went on. "Do you know that twenty-seven dollars is more than some people—adult people, mind you—make in a week? That in some countries people don't make twenty-seven dollars a year? And yet you, all of ten years old, come to me and—"

"But I'll work!" Steely blurted out. "Honest. Every week. I promise."

Mr. Litchstein had been leaning on the counter with his elbows. Now he straightened up and gave Steely a wave of his hand. He was more abrupt than was his nature because he felt a cruel joke was being played on him, though he knew that Steely was serious. Certainly, Mr. Litchstein told himself, he had no reason to feel uncomfortable. Who ever heard of lending a kid so much money?

"Go away, Steely," he said. "Be a nice boy and don't bother me." Wearing a very pained expression, he returned to his customer.

The man said, "Now, as I was trying to say before I was interrupted and insulted—"

"And who insulted you?" asked Mr. Litchstein. "Does the truth hurt so much?"

"As I was saying," persisted the man, taking a

new cup of coffee that the druggist poured for him, "the Jews, the Italians, and the Irish run New York, a fact everybody knows, but when I put it to you I am called Adolf Hitler."

Mr. Litchstein said, "And the man who is now Borough President of Manhattan, one of the most important political jobs in the city, elected by the people—if I am not mistaken, he is a colored man like yourself."

"Yes, and we're very proud of him, too," said the man. "But every time a Negro gets a new job, why is it you white folks start patting yourself on the back and saying to us, 'Look at all the wonderful progress you're making'? You exaggerate that one job out of proportion. It's just window dressing and good old dirty politics. The same people are still running the city."

"You," pronounced the pharmacist very distinctly, "are a political slanderer, a hate-mongerer, a race baiter and a rabble-rouser—"

"There you go again with the insults—"

"Worse, you are a cynic who sneers at progress. Your people are better off today than they ever were, who cares for what reasons? But people like you are never satisfied. You grumble from habit; you bite the hand that feeds you."

The Negro laughed again. Mr. Litchstein frowned darkly and glanced quickly toward the end of the counter. He observed, with a sigh of relief, that Steely had gone. Suddenly he put his hand on the man's shoulder and he laughed, too.

"My friend," he said, "you have a very peculiar sense of humor."

Around Harlem and just about any place else he chose to go, Sugar Boy was considered a sharp guy. He wore the latest style clothes and he had a large red stone on his finger. His hair was conked; in other words, it had been straightened with a hot comb, waved, and set in place with a special hair dressing. It is an expensive proposition to maintain a conk that does not grow ragged around the edges, but Sugar Boy always looked as if he had just left the beauty salon. Not the least of his attractions was his long black Chrysler convertible. Of course he rented garage space, but when he found it necessary to park his car near his apartment, he always paid a boy a quarter to watch it until he came back. Very often this boy was Steely.

On two occasions Steely knew of (and on several others that he did not), city detectives had taken Sugar Boy away in handcuffs. As everyone in the block predicted, Sugar Boy was set free within a few hours. Once he sent Steely with a small package to a house just three blocks away, an errand for which he paid the boy a whole dollar. After that he often stopped to chat with Steely on the street. They always talked about baseball, both agreeing that the Brooklyn Dodgers were far and away the best team. Twice Sugar Boy loaded his Chrysler with Steely and his friends and took them to the ball game, where he bought them loads of popcorn and soda and hot dogs. Naturally Steely liked Sugar Boy. He wondered now why he had not thought of his friend at first.

Sugar's apartment was two rooms and a kitchenette, newly painted and decorated, complete with a blond mahogany television set. Sugar smiled when he opened the door to Steely. "Come on in, man." There was a woman in the room whom Steely had sometimes seen in the Chrysler. She was chestnut brown and buxom. She lay on the couch with her fingers laced across her stomach, her eyes closed.

"Whatcha know, man?" Sugar asked. "What can I do you for?" Sugar's smile was bright and toothy and trimmed in gold. It spoke eloquently of a successful and contented young man looking forward to a quiet evening with his lady friend. The smile went well with the new dacron smoking jacket he was wearing.

Without any preliminaries Steely said, "Will you loan me twenty-seven dollars? I promise to pay you back."

"Will I *what?*"

"Loan me twenty-seven dollars."

Sugar Boy's smile vanished from the room without a trace. The woman on the couch gave a short grunt, sat straight up, and exclaimed, "Damn!" as if there was nothing else to be said for a boy like this one.

"Come on, Steely," Sugar Boy said impatiently. "Who sent you? What do you want?"

Steely was annoyed. "Nobody sent me," he shouted. "I want to borrow some money and I'll work and pay you back."

"Okay, okay," said Sugar Boy. He took a handkerchief from the pocket of his dacron jacket and dabbed at his forehead. Then he ran a hand over his smooth wavy hair. He sank into an easy chair and indicated one for Steely, who declined it without word or gesture. The woman was staring at the boy with amusement and sympathy. She was strangely moved by the grim and darkly serious face.

Sugar Boy said, irrelevantly and with a nervous laugh, "What about those Dodgers over the weekend, huh? Man, that was something!"

At the moment Steely did not care about the Dodgers. He sensed that he was going to be betrayed by his friend. He did not answer, and a weighted silence hung between them.

"How old are you?" Sugar Boy asked suddenly.

"I am ten years old," answered Steely in precise syllables that barely hid his conviction that his age had nothing to do with the matter at hand.

Sugar Boy shifted his position in the easy chair and raised his voice as if he had just decided on a new approach. "Look, kid, if you want a buck for the game tomorrow, I can let you have that." He reached his hand into his trousers pocket and brought out a dollar bill. "Go ahead. Take it." Steely's eyes met Sugar Boy's and held them. He had an urge not to take the money, and he reached for it only after habit had won a brief struggle with his sense of dignity. Reluctantly he put it in his pocket, without yielding an inch on the main point.

"The fact is," Sugar Boy continued hurriedly, feeling silly for having to explain something that was obviously impossible, "I can't lay my hands on that much money right now, sport. It's rough out here in these streets, you know what I mean."

"Yeah," Steely said curtly. He turned and went out of the apartment, leaving behind two thoroughly uncomfortable people.

After a moment Sugar Boy mumbled, "A funny kid, huh?"

"Yeah," said the woman, "a funny kid."

Sugar Boy gave a weak little laugh. "Twenty-seven dollars." He shook his head as if to say he would be damned if he understood what the world was coming to. Then he poured himself a stiff drink.

Outside Steely wandered aimlessly with downcast, sullen eyes. Occasionally he took an angry kick at something loose on the sidewalk. A group of junior-high-school girls marched down the street four abreast. Their white socks were heavy and rolled at the tops. The white and brown of their eyes flashed in the neon lights as the taps on the heels of their flat shoes set up a nervous, metallic chatter. All the pedestrians made way for the girls as they swerved by, singing in young strident voices,

My baby can't mambo, mambo, mambo
My baby can't mambo, mambo, mambo
My baby can't mambo, mambo, mambo
Gonna put my baby down . . .

As Steely turned up Lenox Avenue he reflected that people were not what they should be, that is, straightforward and honest. Sugar Boy was the case in point. He had thought Sugar Boy was his friend, but that was not true at all. Friends helped each other when they were in difficulty. It was an almost sacred, though unspoken, understanding that Sugar Boy had violated. Never again, Steely decided, would he allow himself to be friends with anybody. Nor would he stand guard over Sugar's Chrysler or accept another ticket to the ball game.

He remembered now, as he walked along, that first baseball game—so long ago it seemed the first thing that ever happened to him. He remembered his father's eager eyes as he took a customary punch at him, and his own ducking away and quickly bringing up his guard, the father approving with "Oh, boy," the son throwing punch after punch until both his arms were held behind him.

"Hey, hold up, old boy. I don't want to fight," protested Paul. "Tell me something. Did you ever hear of Jackie Robinson?"

Paul said that Jackie Robinson was a Negro ballplayer, the very first one to play in the Big Leagues. "And you know what, young fellow? We're going out to see him tomorrow. We're going to get a demonstration of what a black man can do when he gets the chance."

It was the longest subway ride he had ever taken, that one over to Brooklyn. When they reached Franklin Avenue they walked out of the station and up a long flight of steps, where they took an elevated train out to Ebbets Field. For the entire trip he sat with his nose pressed against the window, staring out at the squared roofs of the dirty gray apartment houses, feeling strange and important because his mother and father were arguing about him.

"Give the boy a chance," his mother said, "and stop filling his head with all that stuff. He'll have enough trouble in his life without you getting him all hotted up over color and race. I been hearing that nonsense all my life and it ain't never did anybody any good as far as I can see."

"What nonsense?" demanded Paul, his voice suddenly so high and outraged that people turned in their seats to look at him. Mae Brown told him to stop shouting, and he continued in a low, intense voice. "The boy's a Negro and he's got to have something to be proud of. They've cheated him of his heroes. They don't give them to him in school, so you and I have got to do it. You can't grow up without your own heroes, Mae. Every white boy has them, but the black boy's got nothing. George Washington . . . Patrick Henry . . . they're white. A black kid's got to have his own heroes because if he can see himself in history he can see himself in the future."

Mae Brown went on in her flat, dry voice as if he had not spoken. "Heroes, smeroes! I just want him to be like every other boy—"

"But he's not every other boy," Paul interrupted. "He's a particular boy."

"—like every other boy and not mixed up and crazy about this race and politics business. Just leave the boy alone, is all I ask. One of my grandfathers was just like that. He hated white folks so much it ate him up inside and drove him crazy. The white folks are on top and he couldn't do anything about that, so naturally it drove him crazy, hating them the way he did. If he read about where a white man did something wrong to a colored man he couldn't eat for three days. He died, just a mean, shriveled-up little old man. I remember thinking he looked like somebody had poisoned him. It was just all that hate inside of him and not having any way to get rid of it."

"Your grandfather just had a little pride, that's all," said Paul, "which is more than I can say for his granddaughter."

"Pride, my foot!" said Mae Brown, and put an end to the conversation by looking out of the window.

At Ebbets Field when Jackie Robinson ran out onto the diamond Steely saw that it was really true: Jackie was really a colored man. Paul Brown slapped his son on the back and yelled, "There he is! There he is!" When Jackie hit a single Paul stood up and yelled louder than anybody in Brooklyn.

Mae said, "Paul Brown, if you don't sit down and stop making a damn fool of yourself, I'm gonna take these kids and go home. You're disgraceful."

Paul smiled broadly at his wife. "Well, can he play or can't he? I ask you, Mae. Can he play or can't he?"

"Well, I hope he can," she said drily. "Ain't that what they pay him for?"

"God, Mae!" Paul exclaimed in disgust. "You're just plain ignorant."

"Well, that's because I haven't spent all my life in college, like you," she said, ending the conversation in that hard, practical way she had: down-to-earth, colorless and unimaginative, and not half so wonderful as Paul Brown.

That summer Paul and Steely went to the ball game often, but Mae Brown never accompanied them again. Usually Paul and Steely sat in the bleachers or in the lower-priced stands. Everything that Jackie Robinson did thrilled Paul; to him Jackie's playing was not just baseball but life itself. He would say to Steely, "Look at him bouncing on third! Keep your eye on him. He'll steal home if he gets half a chance. You see, the thing that makes him great is that he's always outdoing himself. He knows he's under pressure, so he pushes himself beyond what he thinks he's capable of. That's why he's so beautiful to watch. He's black so he knows he can't give in. He reaches harder for the ball, slides harder into the base. The pressure's on him. Remember that, Fred"—here with his arm around the boy's shoulder and their heads close together, both pairs of eyes watching the man on third—"remember that when you're under pressure, you don't give in, you never give in." Suddenly Paul Brown jumps to his feet and shouts, "There he goes!" And thirty thousand people are standing now to watch the action at the plate. There is a scramble of men and a cloud of dust. The man in the black suit spreads his hands horizontally with the palms downward. Sure enough, Jackie Robinson has stolen home, thereby presenting a dramatic demonstration of Paul Brown's faith.

When Steely turned westward on One Hundred and Twenty-fifth Street he realized that he had not eaten his dinner. He knew he ought to be hungry because it was past eight o'clock. Fishing in his pocket, he brought out the dollar Sugar Boy had given him. It was, he concluded, too far away from twenty-seven to be of any real value, so he let himself be swept along by the pedestrian traffic that was alive with voices and activity. He stopped in front of a Chockfull o' Nuts restaurant and watched the people inside being served by the busy counter workers. After a moment he went in and climbed onto a stool.

When the hot dog and orange drink were set before him, his attention was attracted by the purse of the woman who sat directly across the counter. She was a diminutive person with round, almost comic features. Her quick little eyes were magnified several times by thick rimless glasses. In one hand she held a partially consumed egg salad sandwich and in the other a movie magazine. On the counter in front of her lay her purse, a square black imitation-leather container with a brass clasp. Steely wondered idly if it held as much as twenty-seven dollars. At just this moment the mouselike woman looked up from the magazine and her eyes seemed to catch Steely's. A second later she took the purse from the counter and put it on her lap.

These activities were probably unrelated—looking at Steely and removing her purse. But the boy was all too aware of the direction of his thoughts. He became flustered. Hastily he wiped his mouth with a napkin, slid off the stool, and soon lost himself in the stream of people flowing along One Hundred and Twenty-fifth Street.

four

The idea of snatching a purse was not entirely foreign to Steely, for some of the older boys in The Raiders made a regular practice of it. But he had never thought of snatching one himself; the risk had always seemed too great. His father had told him that a whole life could be ruined by a wrong move, even when you were as young as Steely. If he were sent away to the reformatory he would probably never grow up to be like Frederick

Douglas or Toussaint. Besides, a purse could only be snatched from a woman. He believed that whereas anything was fair between males, or between boys and girls, this was not true of grownup ladies. They seemed a race apart and deserved special consideration. So he had never snatched a purse.

But neither had he ever needed twenty-seven dollars before. At his very immature age Steely had now run head-on into a simple but basic truth: that money is hard come by and it is certainly not to be had for the mere asking. Good friends are reluctant to lend it, and it is not found on the street. It is most scarce when the need is greatest. If you don't have it you must get it, because happiness is impossible without it.

He did not now arrive at these conclusions so clearly but he got the general idea. They necessitated a reconsideration of the views he had held up to that time. It was certainly true that purse-snatching was wrong and that, if caught, he could be sent to jail. But he had to have the twenty-seven dollars, and no one would let him work for it. There were boys in his neighborhood who regularly snatched purses and, so far as Steely knew, none of them was the worse for it. They boasted of their speed. Saturday night, they said, was a good night because women were likely to have larger amounts of money with them.

Everything fell nicely into place. Steely could run faster than any of the purse-snatchers in his neighborhood. And this was Saturday night. Besides, he was not going to make a practice of it. He would get what he needed and that would be the end of it.

Steely did not make up his mind right away. Though he had now readjusted his thinking and morals, the performance of the act itself tended to frighten him. He walked along One Hundred and Twenty-fifth Street, near which the snatchers operated. It was nine o'clock. Blumstein's was long since closed, and all its salesgirls and stock clerks had left. The Five-and-Dime store beside Blumstein's was also securely sealed in darkness. From the penny arcade came the clanking of slot-machine games and the erratic crackle of electric rifles blasting away at the bull's-eye stomach of a revolving brown bear. Lucky Millinder was appearing at the Apollo Theater with his all-star revue. Men and women strollers paused under the lights to stare at the life-sized pictures of near-naked Tonya, a brown Polynesian shake dancer from Valdosta, Georgia. Taxis hummed east and west along this main Harlem thoroughfare. Pedestrians stood poised boldly in the middle of the street as the traffic streaked by on both sides, and when they saw an opportunity they dashed for the sidewalk like soldiers deserting a no man's land. A few doors beyond the Apollo five little brown boys, not one more than eight years old, were setting up a fearsome racket with an assortment of bongo drums, tambourines, and kitchen utensils. All were singing in frantic unison while the smallest of them executed twists, somersaults, and pirouettes with agility in the center of the group.

I'm sailing home, island girl, you'll see,
Just sit on the beach and wait for me.
Some bright morning, one fine day,
I'll lay my anchor and be here to stay.
I'm sailing home, island girl, you'll see,
Just sit on the beach and wait for me.

Steely's senses were stung by the frying hot sausage at the stand at Eighth Avenue where the young men congregate on the corner, colorfully togged out in their best, their restless eyes lustfully following the ebony, bronze, and golden girls who stroll by on the arms of their men, murmuring soft and sugared compliments to those without escorts, loudly bragging to one another of small accomplishments, their empty brashness eloquently bespeaking the murdered dreams, the stunted growth. The Baby Grand Bar stingily spilled ever so little of its amber light through the slanted glass front onto the sidewalk. Frank's Steak House stood like a whore with a genteel past, too self-conscious of its lost dignity. When Steely stopped walking he was at St. Nicholas Avenue, where the street prostitutes, pimps, and hack drivers gather for business. Here at the subway station the boy stopped and stood wondering what to do.

Bold action! That was it. Bold action! He remembered now those conversations his father used to have with Lester Bennett, whom he had met in law school. Lester Bennett was a smooth, smiling yellow man who never raised his voice or made an abrupt gesture. Late at night Paul and Mae and Lester would go into the back room and close the door. The only light Steely could see would be the thin white streak that shot from the keyhole and the purplish mist outside the window. Always the talk was of Negroes. No matter where it started, it ended up on the big problem, the big question. Now, as Steely remembered, it was not a particular conversation but all of them, the voices crossing each other in the darkness, lazy laughter often blending with excited speech; and Steely, hearing and trying to fathom every word, feeling himself in the very core of an exciting movement, for he was a Negro and his father was a Negro and it seemed that Negroes were the most important people in the world.

Bold action. That was what Paul Brown talked about all the time. "We're afraid to act boldly. We hesitate and ask ourselves: How will this reflect on our people? What a question! We've been carrying that cross all these years. As if we were on trial! That's the reason I always liked Jack Johnson or at least what little I know about him. He was before my time. But there was one black man who didn't seem to give a damn what the white folks thought, and they still hate him for it."

"From all I ever heard about him," Mae Brown would say, "he was disgraceful."

"That's all you know about it—"

"Why must Paul stand up when he talks? Sit down and we'll listen."

"He's drunk."

"And I'm right. Now, let me finish and see if you can't see it this way, Lester. We've been getting our freedom in drips and drabs—you know that as well as I do. They've made us toe the line by dangling the great American dream in front of our noses. 'Just be a good boy,' they say, 'and don't cause too much trouble and we'll treat you a little more like a human being.' Am I right or am I wrong?"

"You're right. So what?"

"So maybe it was a great dream, but, hell, man, no dream is good forever! Maybe this one is all washed up. Did you ever think of that? All I ever wanted to do was become a full-fledged American, but now I'm not so sure. The full-fledged white Americans, along with the Russians, are the most hated people on earth. And here we Negroes are, begging for a chance to join them. We're arriving on the scene too late; the world may go up in smoke tomorrow. If we're going to get a little taste of that American dream, we'd better get it *now*. Boldness is what we need. Bold politicians, bold lawyers—that's you and me, Les—and bold bank robbers even."

"I never thought of that before! Why don't we have any good black bank robbers?"

"Now you boys are getting ridiculous and I'm getting sleepy."

"Let's let Mae go to bed. Let's march boldly down to the corner bar and boldly order a nightcap, and I'll show you where you're wrong. You've got more spirit than brains. You forget that there're an awful lot of white people in this country."

"How could I forget that?"

"Settle it when you get to the bar. Good night."

The men would say good night to Mae and go through the dark room and out into the hallway, would go past the boy who lay awake trying to digest the meaning of all he had heard. Always there were new ideas or new ways of looking at old ideas. He had no way of understanding the literal meaning of the words; he felt, rather than comprehended.

Steely laid his plans with as much care as his experience allowed. He would have to select a purse that was held only in the woman's hand—one with no strap. He must be certain there were no cops nearby and that the sidewalk over which he would run would not be too crowded. He would not make the grab until the woman was several yards away from the subway exit; thus he could get a good running start and be moving at top speed when he reached for the bag. For the time being there was nothing to do but wait.

A group of hack drivers was gathered near the newsstand. Their faces reflected the yellowish color of their automobiles and the green tint of the subway lamp. All of them looked tired and sleepy, although they talked with animated voices.

"Where's our white brethren?" asked an elderly man with a dark face and a tweed cap. "I pull up here in the daytime and I can't get on the line for the paddies."

A very tall, ashen yellow man with little eyes answered, "You know those paddy boys are scared to come up to Harlem at night."

"Well, I don't much blame 'em," another said. "Damned if Harlem don't go crazy every Saturday night. I swear, it's a wonder anybody's left alive up here come Sunday."

The ashen yellow man mumbled, "White folks' just as bad, probably worse."

"I don't believe that," protested the other. He was a plump young man with a round face and a voice that whined. "White folks drink and fight and shoot and so on, but honest to God, I don't think they raise as much hell as they do up here in Harlem."

"You mean they're just as bad," the yellow man said, "but you don't think they have as good a time."

"You call it a good time if you want to," said the plump one. "I just call it hell-raising."

"The way I look at it, boys," said the older man with the tweed cap, "is that they're all full of crap. But since I'm a spook, I stick up for the spooks, see. I wouldn't give a paddy the time of day because I figure he's the lowest thing God ever made."

"You're right about that," said the yellow one.

The plump man laughed. "You two just got race prejudice in reverse."

"No such thing." For some reason the old man was becoming angry. He had a toothpick in his mouth and he worked it up and down as he talked. "Prejudice means to make up your mind before you know what it's all about, right? I know because one time I looked it up in the dictionary. Well, I'm fifty-seven years old and I've been around white folks all my life, and if I ain't got a right to judge, ain't nobody."

"What'd the paddies ever do to you, Pop?" asked the plump man.

The elderly man answered emphatically, "Not a damn thing 'cause I always try to stay out of their way and I know damned well they'd better stay out of mine."

The yellow man showed interest in the intensity of the old hack driver's words. He lit a cigarette and looked at the other man through narrowed eyes. "Which ones of 'em you reckon is the worse, Pop?"

"The damned cops, naturally," was the quick answer.

"Cops are cops, black or white," said the plump man.

"No, Pop," said the yellow man. "I mean what races?"

"Well, now, son, I'll tell you," the other began as though he had given the question a great deal of thought. "The Italians is rough, the Jews is smart, and the Irish is dumb, but they all manage to get along—"

"The Negroes and the Puerto Ricans must be the dumbest," interrupted the plump man, "because they ain't getting along at all."

The rumble of arriving trains below the surface of the street ended the conversation. The men went to their cars, and soon all of them were employed. Other cabs parked at the curb and another group of drivers formed near the newsstand. This was a younger gathering, and their talk was of women. Steely continued to wait. In the crowd there had been only one purse that had been safe to snatch, but he had hesitated too long.

There was one unescorted woman in the next group that emerged from the subway station. She was short and dumpy and wore a blue flowered dress. In her hand was a small black cloth bag.

Instantly Steely was off. When he passed her he was running as fast as he could. His fingers closed firmly on the bag as he snatched it from her hand.

All she saw was a small dark figure quickly disappearing. Steely had turned the corner and was running westward on One Hundred and Twenty-sixth Street before she realized what had happened. Steely heard the scream, but already he was far away.

"I've got it!" Steely whispered to himself. "I've got it!" he thought over and over again.

There were only a few people on the street in this residential block, and none of them paid any attention to him. He felt exultant. He had acted boldly. He had done a daring deed and now he was safe.

But suddenly there were footsteps behind him. They were heavy, they struck the sidewalk less often than his own, but they came nearer. Steely tried to pull away from them, to widen the gap, but he couldn't. The footsteps seemed right behind him now.

Steely stopped abruptly and jumped off the sidewalk into the street. The man behind him was so large and was moving so fast that he had to go several steps farther before he could stop. He whirled on the boy.

"Come 'ere, boy!" he ordered, holding out one of his hands as if to hypnotize Steely. A huge brown man of middle age, he was breathing heavily. "Gimme that damned purse, y'hear?"

He was panting heavily. The boy was prepared when the man lunged at him suddenly. He ducked back to the sidewalk and ran on in the direction he had been going. Soon the footsteps were after him again, but now they were tired and began to recede in the distance.

Steely cut up Old Broadway, ran a block, then headed back toward Amsterdam Avenue. There he merged with the Saturday night crowd. His heart was thumping loudly. He was safe and the purse was in his pocket, snug against his thigh.

But there was nothing in it! That is, there was nothing like the twenty-seven dollars he needed. There were two one-dollar bills, a stick of lipstick, an eyebrow pencil, and a package of doublemint gum. There were letters, tissues, keys, and identification papers. There were all kinds of things, but there was no twenty-seven dollars.

He had stopped to examine the purse near a dark playground. He pushed the two dollars into his pocket and angrily flung the bag over the fence.

Now Steely had to run again, and he sped as fast as his tired legs could carry him, down the hill eastward into the heart of Harlem, away from the playground and the purse, away from the scene of his sharp disappointment and newly born frustration. It hadn't occurred to him that the purse might not contain the money he wanted. So desperate was his need and so great was the risk he had taken that there hadn't been the slightest doubt that the purse would contain exactly twenty-seven dollars, not a penny more or less. As he ran, his mind churned with wild thoughts and images. He pictured his mother waiting for him impatiently, certainly exasperated by now. He imagined the obstacles he had yet to overcome this night in order to get what he wanted. His body was hotly charged with a growing sense of urgency. When he came to a massive gray-stone church on St. Nicholas Avenue, he sat on the steps and tried to pull himself together.

five

Steely caught a downtown bus and sat next to an open window. He looked out but saw nothing. His mind was turned inward where memories and feelings were stored. His thoughts were not of the great general world because he already had a concrete image of that. The world, as he saw it, was divided into two races, Negroes and white people. Between them there was an exciting contest, and he, Steely, was fortunate enough to have been born on the side of right. The white people were on top now, but this situation was only temporary. Ultimately Negroes would triumph, and Steely expected to make a great contribution to the final victory. It was all very simple; for him the outside world was not complicated at all.

But in personal matters he felt lost and completely adrift. Even now, so many months after Paul's disappearance, Steely was shocked and uncomprehending. Nothing that had happened made any sense to him. He had conjured up a hundred explanations for what had happened, but not one of them could put his searching mind at rest or ease the excruciating sense of loss and hurt. He had even tried to make himself hate Paul, but he was too possessed by a bruised love for his father to admit of any hate. Besides, he could not yet exercise sufficient control over his furious and clashing emotions.

It was wanting to understand so much and yet understanding nothing—this was the salt added to the wound of having suddenly lost the person whom he loved above all others. He asked himself a hundred questions and each unanswered one became a sharp knife that seemed to cut at his soul.

His simple concept of love had not been outraged; it had merely been overridden. No matter how he tried to mold it in his mind, it could not be made to fit the present situation. To him love was the most natural and easy thing, something you could almost take for granted. He loved Paul and Mae Brown for very obvious reasons. He had always loved them and had almost always felt that they loved him. Why should it not be the same between the two of them? Steely had by now discovered that adult love was a different thing entirely, but there was no way in which he could understand why this should be. Nor could he begin to perceive the different forms assumed by such love, or its eternally changing character.

His hurt would not have been so deep had he not felt so much alone. His extreme dependence upon Paul had left him with a void that no other person or activity could fill. He instinctively knew that his mother could be of no help to him, so he did not turn to her. Though there was love, there was really no medium of communication between them. His ideas on almost everything had originated with Paul. He had tried to be like his father and think like him. Never had there been a teacher or a boy on the street who had for even one moment threatened to replace Paul in Steely's esteem. So now, with Paul gone, there was small wonder that he felt so utterly alone.

As he scrambled around in this psychological and emotional state he uncovered something that was to prove very important. Now, for the first time, he began to see contradictions between what people say and what they do. In searching for so many answers, he had shaken his own faith in his father. When Paul Brown had talked about great Negroes, Steely had looked at Paul with wide, credulous eyes and pictured those Negroes in Paul's image. Now, as Steely recalled each little incident, he began to believe that Paul Brown had done some things those heroes would not have done. He felt vaguely disappointed with his father. This embryo stirring of criticism had never been allowed to approach the surface. He even felt a trifle guilty for allowing such thoughts to cross his mind. But once there, they would not go away. Against his wishes he was becoming a sensitive, yet ruthless, observer of the gap between the word and the deed, between the ideal and the accomplished fact. Thus his instant condemnation and banishment, without appeal, of Mr. Litchstein and Sugar Boy from the ever shrinking circle of people whom he liked.

He was disturbed now as he tried to apply the

yardstick to incidents long past. He was remembering those nights when his father would stay away until very late; then he would hear Paul's thudding footsteps on the stairs. Sometimes Paul would trip but he never fell. Steely would hear the squeaking of the banisters and know that his father was holding on while he gathered strength for another try at reaching the fifth floor where they lived. Having gained the hallway and groped his way along the dark passage, Paul would stand outside the door fumbling for his keys, mumbling incoherently. When the door finally swung open the mumbling would cease abruptly as he concentrated on not disturbing the children.

Once in the other room, he would start to take off his clothes. Mae's voice would suddenly drone with dull contempt in the darkness:

"It beats me why you come home at all."

"My God, woman! Don't you ever sleep?" Paul's words would be thick and blurred. With a heavy sigh he would sit on the bed and take off his shoes. Each of them would strike the floor with a dull, inconclusive thud. "Les and I were studying and we stopped for a drink, that's all."

"What are you and Les doing? Drinking your way through law school?"

"Don't worry about it. Don't worry about it."

"What are you trying to be? A playboy like Les?" Her voice would be brittle and trembling. "He's young with no responsibilities. You've got responsibilities—"

"I know. You keep reminding me."

"Well, you shouldn't have to be reminded."

For a moment they would be silent. Then, almost electrically, Mae's tight, trembling words would crackle in the darkness. "Are you running around with women, Paul?"

"Oh, God—"

"Don't 'oh, God' me. What are you doing, buying them, or do you and Les spend all your free time hunting them in bars?"

"Look, Mae—" Paul would shout.

"Don't wake up the kids—"

"Well, cut it out, will you?" Paul's voice would be heavy with disgust. "Jesus, I go out and have a drink—maybe a little too much, so what?—but I come home and get accused of every damned thing that comes into your head. What's the matter with you?"

"I'm sorry, Paul."

"Well, you ought to be."

Another silence would fill the apartment while they both waited.

"Paul."

"What is it?"

"What's the matter? Are you having trouble at school? They say the first year in law school—"

"I'm not having any trouble. At least no more than I'd expect."

"Well, why do you drink so much?"

Paul would not answer.

"What are you doing to us, Paul?"

Silence.

"Good night, Mae. I don't feel like talking. I'm tired and I'm drunk and I'm sleepy. So good night."

"Good night, Paul."

For a long time Steely would lie awake, knowing that both of them were still awake, and wondering what they were thinking.

When he thought of the great Negro leaders, he could not envision them as drunk. He tried very hard, he thought of all kinds of explanations, but the pieces of the picture never seemed to fit together.

There were many such nights and, as he recalled them, they blended together, leaving a single impression of wonder and sadness. But one night stood by itself, stamped indelibly in his memory. It was at the end of Paul's first year in law school. Steely was sound asleep when the voices woke him. They were muffled and distant in the slumbering building.

"Mark, you sure you got him?"

"I've got him. It's just so damned dark out here."

"There ought to be a light."

"The place is at the end of the hallway here."

"Come on, Paulus, old boy. Just a little further."

"Goddamn, he's heavy!"

"Don't you let Paulus fall."

"Vickie, for Christ's sake, keep quiet. Why the hell do we all have to crowd up here anyway? Especially you, Vickie."

"God, it stinks up here."

"This feels like a door."

"This is it."

Steely could remember the heavy knocks at the door. He sat up in bed gasping for breath, realizing only then that he had not breathed since he woke up. Now his heart thumped like the knocks. The light went on in the other room, and after a moment his mother came out, tying the belt of her bathrobe under which her stomach bulged with the baby that was to be Carol Ann. Her eyes were frightened as she rushed to the door crying, "I'm coming, I'm coming!"

Except for his father and Lester Bennett, they were all white. A slight blond man with eyeglasses was helping Lester carry Paul, who hung limply between them, his arms over their shoulders. And there were three women, their white faces whiter in the naked light, their eager eyes darting around the cluttered room, taking in the huddled form of Robby on his cot against the far wall, staring with unconcealed curiosity at Steely, who stared back with open hostility.

Lester said, "We're sorry to bother you at this hour, Mae, but we thought we'd better bring Paul home."

"Paulus," said one of the women. "Not Paul. When did he stop being Paulus?"

Lester groaned. "Oh, for God's sake!"

The blond man spoke sharply. "Shut up, Vickie!"

"Bring him in here," said Mae Brown.

The two men carrying Paul followed her into the other room, where Steely heard them letting his father down onto the bed. Now the three women walked into the room.

"My God, this place is awful. No wonder Paulus—"

"Vickie, don't be as much of a bitch as we know you can be."

The third woman was slender and dark haired. She sat on the arm of the overstuffed chair. She lifted a pale hand with long white fingers to her head. "Jesus, what a party! I won't be able to think straight for a week."

"You're Paulus's little boy, aren't you?"

The woman called Vickie was leaning toward him. Her smile was wide and red-lipped, and her teeth were white and even. But Steely did not like her smile, and it never occurred to him to answer her.

"If I were a sculptor," she said, "I would do your head in bronze. Do you know that?"

He wondered what she was talking about. He stared at her but he still did not speak.

His mother and the two men came out of the other room. "It's our fault, Mae, honestly," Lester was saying. "Honest to God, if I had dreamed something like this would happen . . . well, it's all my fault. Paul kept trying to come home but—well, you know how it is when you've been drinking—we just wouldn't let him."

All the white people voiced their agreement with what Lester was saying. Steely had never heard him talk so loudly before.

"—and the next thing you know," the blond man picked up the story, his voice suddenly high as the words gushed over each other, "poor Paul is out on his feet. But really you can't put him in the doghouse, really, because it was our fault and Paul isn't used to running with us."

"We were trying to cheer Paulus up."

His mother looked at the woman called Vickie. The look was long and strange and hard, as if Mae Brown had always known the woman and had always hated her. So Steely, too, looked at Vickie, a tall woman with shining eyes and soft, neatly clipped black hair. He saw a pretty woman like the movie stars with their clean features and their white skins and that mist of silver and gold that follows them. He had never expected to see such a woman in his home, nor could he have said why he felt afraid of her and why he disliked her so much.

"And what did he have to be cheered up for?" Mae Brown asked in an even voice.

The blond man moved uneasily. He put his hand on Vickie's arm and said, "Come on. Let's go."

Vickie ignored him. "Because he flunked it. You didn't know, did you? Yes, poor Paulus flunked out of school."

"Oh," was all Mae Brown said, but it was hushed and low.

"As a matter of fact," Vickie went on, "we all flunked out. At the end of the first year they have general house cleaning and we got swept out, that's all. But it didn't make that much difference to me because I don't really care. It was just an idea I had. Les, he didn't really care either. He wouldn't have made a good lawyer or a good anything, for that matter." She gave all of her companions a sweeping look that was almost drowsy with scorn. "Neither would any of us. But Paulus—" She shook her head. "You'll never know how much he wanted the law. I know, though. He told me and I listened."

"Well, thank you for telling me," said Mae in the same even tone.

"Any time," Vickie said. She turned and almost stumbled as she walked toward the door. The blond man steadied her.

"I'm sorry about all this, Mae," said Lester, lingering behind the others, who now seemed to be rushing out of the room. "You know how Paul was, how much he wanted to—"

"You talk about him like he was dead, Les," said Mae.

"I'm sorry," Lester said again; then he, too, turned and rushed from the room. Mae Brown closed the door and listened as they stumbled through the hallway.

It was Lester's voice that was heard almost immediately. "Goddamn it, Vickie. I ought to slap your head sideways."

"What did I do?"

"You were just your own sweet self," said one of the women, "and that was what we were afraid of."

Suddenly Vickie began to sing in a loud voice:

"We're six little failures who've lost our way
Bah . . . bah . . . bah . . ."

"Shut her up, for Christ's sake!"

Somebody stumbled. "They ought to put some light in here."

"It stinks to high heaven."

"Thank God for slum clearance," said Vickie.

Then they were feeling their way down the stairs

and their voices faded away. Mae Brown had been standing all this time with her back to the door, her hand over her mouth as if to keep down a scream. Now she became aware that Steely was awake and watching her. She reached quickly for the cord in the center of the room and snapped out the light. But even after Steely heard the switch, in that instant before the light swiftly vanished, he saw her face. The naked light was absorbed by her dark, terrified eyes, the full anguish and the torment written there; and just before she closed the door to the other room Steely heard the sound she made. It was a sudden, weak cry, a whimper, that only half conveyed the hurt she felt.

When Steely reached Ninety-sixth Street he changed buses and rode crosstown through Central Park to the East Side. At Madison Avenue he walked southward into a part of the city that was very different from his Harlem. Here there were small, neat shops, groceries, and delicatessens. In the side streets pretty apartment houses with awnings and trimmed hedges spilled warm light through the blinds of the windows and onto the clean sidewalks. Steely was intimidated by the quiet and reserve of the community. He avoided looking directly into the faces of the people he passed in the street. If he had not been driven by his purpose he would have retraced his steps to Harlem.

It was past ten o'clock. He hardly dared think of his mother and how angry she must be. In his mind he tried to picture whether she was standing up or sitting down as she waited for him. How did she intend to beat him? With the strap or with her hands? He decided that she would use the strap because this would be a long beating and she wouldn't want to hurt her hands. In the same rigid manner with which he judged others, he now judged himself. He was guilty; there was no question of it; and he deserved the worst possible punishment from his mother. Under any circumstances he would have had to submit to the punishment physically, but this admission of his guilt would not allow him to bow to it morally and psychologically. He could not hope to escape the beating, but if he could recover the money, he would, to some extent at least, compensate for his guilt.

Two white boys on bicycles passed him in the street. Both of them pumped laboriously as if they had come a long way and were tired. This was the kind of thing Steely had been waiting for. Keeping to the sidewalk, he followed them, trotting just fast enough to watch them and yet not attract their attention. After several blocks he became tired and wanted to stop. The muscles of his legs trembled, throwing hot and cold waves up his thighs. Then his legs were suddenly numb and his breath came in gasps. He knew he could not run another block. Then the boys turned into Eighty-eighth Street. Steely slowed to a walk. Just as he had hoped, one of the bicycles was in the front areaway of an apartment house. It leaned on its own kickstand just a few feet from the vestibule.

Steely walked past the areaway and glanced at the bicycle. It was a Silver Streak with lots of chromium on it. In the stores it sold for at least fifty dollars.

Steely was surprised and pleased by his own calmness. He did not have the same tightness in his chest that had been there when he snatched the purse. He thought of the guys in the movies who calmly light cigarettes before they pull a big job.

The circumstances seemed favorable. He could see no one sitting out of doors. He walked around the block and then turned back into Eighty-eighth Street. The bicycle was still in the areaway. He put a hand on the gate, pushed it open, and went in.

Holding the bicycle erect by its handle bars, Steely reached down quickly with his other hand and pulled the kickstand quietly into its catch.

Quietly he walked with the bicycle through the gate. Quietly he pushed it over the sidewalk into the street. Then he gave himself a good running start and leaped into the seat. He now owned a bike.

six

There was one boy in The Comanche Raiders who was known by everybody for blocks around as the "Bike King." This was fifteen-year-old Junior Robinson, who loved bicycles and seemed to know all about them. His own was thought to be the handsomest outfit in Harlem. It had colored lights, battery-powered horns, fur tails, and an extensive multicolored collection of reflectors. Running across the handle bars were all the flags of the United

Nations, and only recently he had added a portable radio powered by a generator attached to the front wheel.

Once Junior Robinson had put Steely on his cross bar and ridden him down to Ninety-sixth Street. There he had told Steely to take the bike back home by himself, and then he had walked away. As Steely had pedaled homeward the older boy had overtaken him, riding a bike that Steely had never seen before. Then Steely had understood that he had just helped Junior Robinson pull a job. When they reached home Junior had dismantled the new bicycle. He said he always swiped bikes from the "gray" boys because when he walked along their streets he could be sure of finding one that wasn't locked. He confided to Steely that he got a good price for all the bikes he obtained in this manner. He had very good relations with a junk dealer near the East River who dealt in all such merchandise. Junior had cautioned Steely not to try the same thing because the younger boy's legs were too short and he could not pedal fast enough.

Although only a few months had passed since he had received this warning, Steely felt he had grown considerably. He intended to hunt up the Bike

King, who would help him sell the Silver Streak. He did not expect the older boy to refuse, now that the stealing of the bicycle was an accomplished fact.

He wanted to go north on Park Avenue, but he changed his mind when he spotted a police car on the next corner. He decided to ride farther east and turn homeward on Lexington Avenue. He knew he would be in Avenger territory, but he felt he would be relatively safe because he intended riding only along its fringe. If he could ride unmolested for eight short blocks he would be able to cross Ninety-sixth Street. There he would be in the safer neighborhood of The Conquistadores, with whom The Comanche Raiders had recently signed a peace pact. Then he would ride westward into his own territory.

But Steely had no way of knowing of an event of the preceding day that was to have considerable influence on his plans. On the previous morning two boys had fought over a girl at a soda fountain on Ninety-sixth Street. That would have been the end of it had one of the boys not been white and the other Puerto Rican. For almost twenty hours the blocks near Ninety-sixth Street had been the scenes of sporadic but violent clashes between groups of four and five boys. Finally the leaders of both sides had met and agreed to make war on each other this very night. Although the trouble had originated among the older boys, whole neighborhoods of youths were now involved. In an organized war boys down to the age of nine or ten were expected to participate. Girls' groups played an important part in the strategy: they concealed weapons in their clothing and gave them to the boys only when they drew near the scene of the "rumble" that had been agreed upon by both sides.

Thus it happened that when Steely reached Ninety-fifth Street, only a block away from the battle spot, he almost ran into the rear of a large formation of Avengers.

He heard them yelling just before he saw them—a group of boys moving threateningly toward the other corner. Steely braked the Silver Streak and spun around. But the tires screamed over the pavement.

"Hey, lookit the boogie!"

"Where the hell that sonuvabitch come from?"

Ride, Steely, ride!

On foot and bicycle, a group of boys detached themselves from the main body and hurried into the chase. Frantically Steely pushed the Silver

Streak back over the few yards to the corner, where he turned downhill toward Second Avenue. He almost fell off trying to pedal the slack out of the chain, but he managed to stay on. Instantly he had a new plan. He was now pedaling toward the East River. He would turn north at Second Avenue and try to go west across Ninety-sixth Street.

He pedaled furiously down the long block. He knew he had outdistanced those on foot but that the bicycles were still following him.

"Hey, Comancheeeeee!"

"Hey, you black Comancheeee! Hold up!"

"Yeah, we want to talk to you."

For the first time since he had bought it, Steely wished he were not wearing his Comanche jacket. Its luminous green was visible several blocks away.

"Hey, Comancheeee!"

Ride, Steely, ride!

He sped across Ninety-sixth Street and almost collided with the side of a bus. The boys behind him were probably bigger, since they were gaining, but he felt he would be safe because they would not follow him very far into Conquistador territory.

Ride, Steely, ride!

Away he pedaled. Pain dragged at his thigh muscles. He wished he were Superman so that his strength would never give out.

Suddenly he was filled with dismay. He had forgotten that all the buildings had recently been torn down on both sides of Second Avenue to make way for a new housing project. The street was dark and empty except for the cars speeding past. He had no hope of help or protection from grownups who might be on the street. No wonder the Avengers behind him had not given up the chase. He thought of turning toward Lexington Avenue, but he would have to pedal uphill and they would surely catch him. Nor could he turn to First Avenue. Nobody lived over there. He had to keep going forward.

Sweat burned his eyes. He tasted the salt at the edges of his mouth and his chest felt like a hot dry oven. The cobblestones were slowing him down. He heard only the sounds of the bicycles behind him—the clacking of loose lights and horns—and his own heavy breathing.

Keep going, Steely, keep going!

His whole body ached. The bikes behind drew closer. The boys no longer called to him but gave all their strength to their pedaling. He knew he must not give up, as Paul had said, must never give up, but even as he swore this, he knew he would be caught.

One of the Avengers rolled past Steely and came to a sudden halt a few yards ahead, blocking Steely's path. He braked his bike and stood beside it, panting. The other boys rolled up and stopped, too. All of them were two or three years older than Steely. For a full minute nobody said anything because they were all winded.

The boy who had blocked Steely's way seemed to be the leader. He said hoarsely, "Hey, Jack, didn't you hear us calling you?"

Steely did not answer.

"Hey, man, dig that crazy pair of wheels he's riding!"

"Man, that's pretty!"

"Yeah, that's a Silver Streak!"

"That's real pretty, Jack."

"Crazy, man, crazy."

They chanted these words as if they were a part of a ritual. Steely knew that nothing he could say would make any difference, so he kept quiet.

"What did you say, Jack?" asked the leader. "Did I hear you say you're gonna be nice and give us this crazy bike?"

A chubby boy with black curly hair laid his bike

down on the street and walked over to Steely. He gave Steely a stiff shove that separated him from the Silver Streak and landed him on the ground. As he got up, Steely wondered what he could do. The chubby boy was holding his bicycle.

Another boy taunted, "Oh, he's a real little Comanche, he is."

"Oh, I'll bet he's gonna grow up to be real tough."

A slender boy in motorcycle boots laid his bike down. "Come on, let's see how tough Amos 'n' Andy is," he said.

Steely was knocked down and kicked.

He got up and swung at the boy who was closest to him. It was a wild blow, and the boy, the chubby one, struck Steely solidly on the side of his head. Steely was staggered. For a moment he couldn't see. He stood shakily in the center of the ring of Avengers.

"One thing about Little Black Sambo—he don't cry, huh?"

Their voices were almost leisurely, as if they were playing a tiresome game.

"Hey, Peewee, I bet you can't make Sambo cry."

"Let's see about that."

Steely hardly felt the blow, but he was knocked to the cobblestones. He just sat there. He was so weak and dispirited that he had no will to get up.

"Amos 'n' Andy ain't crying yet."

"Shame on you, Peewee."

Suddenly nervousness began to overtake them. Their voices became tense and worried.

"Man, let's clear outa here before some of them spiks come along."

"Yeah, let's hit back across Ninety-sixth."

"Yeah, man."

"Here, Peewee, grab the other handle of this bike."

"Yeah, man!"

"Wahooo!"

"So long, Boogie!"

"Yeah, man!"

"Take it easy, Amos 'n' Andy."

"Wahooo!"

They pedaled away swiftly. Steely did not look after them. He moved to the curbstone and sat there without moving.

He was not angry. In his mind there was not even a thought of the Avengers or of the bruises they had given him. He was thinking of the still-missing twenty-seven dollars, of how long the night was and of how much more of it loomed before him.

seven

Steely knew it would not be easy for him to roll a drunk. He would need both patience and luck. The larger boys could take more chances because they could rely on their strength in case the unexpected developed; that is to say, if the drunk resisted.

Once Steely had seen Shotgun and Red Louis roll a drunk under the One Hundred and Fifteenth Street overpass. The man had come staggering along the street and they had offered to help him get home safely. He had grumbled and tried to wave the boys away. Then he had wobbled on, with them following closely. They had caught up with him under the overpass, gone through his pockets before he knew what had happened, shoved him hard against the large damp stones of the tunnel wall, then run away toward the safety of the crowd on One Hundred and Sixteenth Street.

But of course Steely was too small to try such a thing. There were other ways he had heard of, though he had never seen any of them in practice. Now it was after midnight. Soon the drunks would stagger out of the saloons. Most of them would be able to get home under their own power, but a few would fall to the sidewalk and lie there until the next morning. Others would find shelter and sleep in dark unknown hallways. From the pockets of one or several of these, Steely was determined to obtain the money he needed.

He was in Harlem again. With the new plan his hope and spirit returned. He was tired, for he had never been out so late, but he had no thought of giving up. Tense and excited, he was completely single-minded.

This neighborhood was like his own. Most of the numberless apartments were dark now. But in the windows above the street sat the old people keeping their gray, lonely vigil because they could not sleep. They were exiles in a cramped, busy world that had no time for them.

The street was all shadows and blackness, relieved by the tepid white light from an occasional lamp. Steely searched from block to block. No one walked the street. Were it not for the passing cars, he might have been the only person in the world. It was so still and quiet.

The boy should have been afraid but he was not. It was a new and strange passion that possessed him, and its embrace was almost pleasurable. He was committed to a cause, an objective, and he could not stop himself.

But he stopped suddenly just as he was nearing a street lamp. He had heard the faint creaking of rusty wheels. Then, low and far away, but distinctly:

Cina, cina, cina,
Dogwé sang, cina lo-gé

Steely had never seen Black Papa at night. As the shriveled old man pushed his cart into the orbit of the lamplight, his dirty gray stubble of beard and matted hair glowed luminously white. His black skin showed ashen, and his eyes seemed darker and deeper than ever they had by daytime. When the old man was directly under the lamp they seemed not to be eyes at all but empty sockets like the two top holes in a grotesque Halloween mask.

Steely held his breath and trembled as Black Papa passed within a few feet, droning his incantation. It was only a simple prayer, Steely's father had told him, a prayer to a Haitian sea god, but the very strangeness of the sounds stirred the boy's imagination. Here in the night, in this strange and empty place, the words seemed full of black foreboding.

Steely hurried away in the opposite direction, suddenly frightened and desperate for a reason he did not know. He was being chased by evil things. Any moment they would snatch out and envelop him in darkness and gloom. Only when he came to a well-lighted avenue did he feel safe.

But for his purpose he had to keep in the dark streets. He forced himself to turn into another dimly lighted block and walk through it.

This was one of those lively Harlem neighborhoods. Here and there men and women languished on steps and in doorways. They were drinking cold beer and cheap wine, relating dirty jokes in loud, uncouth voices, and ribbing one another with explosive, raucous laughter. Steely was passing in front of one such group when a man shouted out of a window several stories overhead.

"For God's sake!" he cried in exasperation, "will you people shut up and go to bed, or at least move down the street and give decent people a chance to sleep?"

A woman in the group got up suddenly. In the faint light Steely could see her twisted, tormented features set in a drunken face, her eyes ablaze like a cat's. She yelled back in a high, hysterical voice:

"You shut up yourself, you old bastard, and mind your own goddamn business!"

In one impulsive sweep of her arm she heaved her bottle up toward the man, losing her balance as she did so, falling among her friends. The bottle crashed against the building and glass fragments began falling into the street. The group of people huddled into the doorway. A man laughed and said, "Damn, woman, ain't no use trying to kill *us* just because you're mad at him."

Steely ran to the corner and across the street. Now he was not very afraid. The sudden noises and the suggested violence of Saturday night created a bizarre, chilling effect, but he clung tenaciously to his purpose.

Then he saw a drunk. The man stumbled from the avenue into the block where Steely was. He wobbled from the steps of the tenements to the parked cars, then back across the sidewalk to the steps again. In order to avoid notice, the boy stood still against a fence. Steely could see the drunk's face. He was of a dark complexion that seemed purple in the wan light. His eyes stared straight ahead as if naked will power alone kept them open. His lips sagged, revealing several gold teeth. He caught sight of Steely and lunged slowly toward the boy with his arms outstretched.

"Hiya, little boy."

He was moving like a figure in a slow-motion picture. Steely darted away and the man fell heavily against the fence where the boy had been standing. He braced himself, groaned and shook his head, not certain that he had seen a little boy at all. Then he lurched forward along the sidewalk again. Steely followed like a frightened animal, waiting anxiously for the man to fall.

But in front of one tenement building the drunk stopped and blinked up at the address. He swayed on his feet and gave a loud, long yawn. Then he seemed to fall toward the doorway and disappear.

Steely felt wild frustration. The man lived in the building! But perhaps this was the wrong house. Maybe he would lie down in the hallway. Steely ran up the steps and into the vestibule. The door to the apartment at the rear of the ground floor hallway was just closing. The man was nowhere in sight.

Out on the street again Steely felt keen disappointment but some relief. He walked along half-heartedly, doubting himself, wondering if he would have shrunk back at the last moment, too afraid to do what had to be done.

"Hello, young fellow."

A white man had pulled his car to the curb and now drove it slowly along beside Steely. He was smiling.

"I said hello, young fellow."

His voice seemed to smile too. Steely had never heard a voice so friendly. But it had come suddenly and it seemed out of place on a dark Harlem street. He quickened his step almost to a run. The car drew up beside him again.

"Come here, little boy. I won't hurt you."

Steely did not stop. The man could not fool him;

he was one of those queers. Steely had heard the boys talk. A queer was a man who acted like a woman and did dirty things. You were not supposed to have anything to do with them. Steely got ready to break into a run.

"What are you afraid of?" the man asked quickly. "I won't hurt you. How would you like to make some money?"

Steely hesitated, then stopped. He turned and looked at the man with mixed fear, hostility, and reluctant interest.

"Come here so I can talk to you. You don't want me to yell all over the street, do you?"

Steely took two steps toward the car but held back as if he might run any minute. He was afraid the man would open the door and grab him. The man was thirtyish. He had a long face that was as friendly as his smile and his voice. Steely was sure he was rich because the car was a long new Cadillac. It had been polished to such a gloss that it sparkled even in the dark. Surely a man who owned such a car could easily afford twenty-seven dollars.

"Now, wouldn't you like to make some money?" the white man asked.

Steely was thinking that he would not have to roll a drunk after all; he would get the money from this queer. Nobody else would know about it. Just once he would do whatever it was this queer man did, and he would never do it again. In answer to the question he nodded his head slowly.

"Of course you would," affirmed the man excitedly, as if to punctuate Steely's unspoken words. "Of course you would."

He let his eyes rest for a long moment on the boy's face. Steely thought he was expected to say something but he didn't know what. He felt uncomfortable and wanted to fidget but he stood still.

"What's your name?"

"Steely."

It was the first word he had spoken in several hours. The sound of his voice surprised him; he could hardly believe he had answered. It was as if the man's warm manner and smile had charmed the word out of him.

"Ah, Steely," breathed the man with satisfaction. He lowered his voice and the next words came out unctuously. "Steely, how would you like to make a whole dollar?"

"I don't want a dollar," Steely said bluntly. "I want twenty-seven dollars."

The smile on the man's face vanished; a frown was there for the quickest moment, then the smile stole back. "Well, well, you *are* an enterprising little chap, aren't you?" he said. "Ha ha ha," he laughed. "Well, Steely, if you would like to make twenty-seven dollars, you just come and take a little ride with me—"

But already he was speaking to Steely's fleetly disappearing figure. The boy had seen the troubled frown and recognized it. In that instant he had thought of Mr. Litchstein and Sugar Boy and the violated trust. This man would have been like that, too. So he ran as fast as he could, though he knew he was not being followed.

eight

At Central Park Steely walked under the tall trees that at night cast deep shadows and blanket the park with heavy gloom. He moved over the sidewalk just outside the stone wall. Here and there a boy and a girl fumbled with each other in the darkness. Under a street lamp two elderly women sat in stern, animated discussion of family and neighborhood affairs. An occasional car sped through the hush, paused for a red light, then rushed on. The stillness was profound. Steely stepped lightly, as if fearing that a scuffle of his shoe might strike a spark that would explode the highly inflammable night. He sat down when he came to an empty bench tucked away in the shadows.

Now he realized he was tired. He wanted to close his eyes and sleep. He mumbled, "I can't. I've got too much to do." But a few moments later his chin was on his chest and his eyes were closed. The city murmured around him, but he did not hear it.

He was neither asleep nor awake. He was back in that confusing time after the night when they had brought Paul Brown home, remembering how just a few days later Carol Ann was born. Steely was the one who had run down for a taxi. The first two drivers had refused to wait when they found out about the baby because they said they did not want their cars bloodied up. But the third driver was a good guy who had walked up the five flights and helped Paul carry Mae down the stairs. Robby had set up an awful wail, and Paul had told Steely to stay at home and look after his younger brother. Carol Ann had come too soon, they said, and they had to leave her at the hospital for almost a month.

Even then she was the tiniest baby Steely had ever seen.

And all the time his father was so different. It worried Steely no end, the way Paul Brown never talked much any more, just came and went, working two jobs, now that he was not studying law; just came and went with a quiet, subdued look about the eyes that the boy had never seen there before. Paul smiled sometimes, but sadly. Sometimes he laughed, too, but not in the bold, free way he had before, the laughter ringing off the plastered walls, seeming to dominate everything it touched. Nor did he ever put his hand on Steely's shoulder and say all those wonderful and fantastic things, using his hands and arms to draw pictures in the air.

During this period Steely once said, "Let's go out to Ebbets Field next week, Pop, and see Jackie."

"A good idea," Paul said. "If I can find time we'll go."

But of course he forgot all about it. It just never crossed his mind again, and Steely came to know that the Dodgers and Jackie Robinson were not so important any more. Steely told himself he would be like this new Paul Brown and not even think about baseball and such things. He would be quiet like his father, and sad, too, and think the same somber thoughts, even if he did not know what they were.

Steely knew they should have been happy. His mother was no longer working at the laundry. Now she was at home all the time with Carol Ann and Robby. There was plenty to eat, and Steely came home from school for lunch every day. The house was clean because his mother made the place look shining. Steely had never imagined the two rooms could look so nice.

But something was wrong. It was in everything about the house. He had his ways of knowing; they could not fool him. It wasn't only the way his father looked and acted, it was his mother, too. The way she said, "Hi, Paul," when he came in from work, just like that, quiet and polite as if they hardly knew each other. Even when Paul came home late with that red look around his eyes, when Steely could tell that he had been drinking, she would say, "Hi, Paul," and never raise her voice; and he would say, "Hello," and go straight to bed. She would go back to what she had been doing, just as if he had not come in at all. Steely kept thinking it was as if something were dead, but he did not know why he thought this. He would turn his face to the wall, not wanting to look at his mother's face, knowing instinctively that he would not like what he saw there.

Sitting beside the park wall, Steely was not dreaming now, or remembering exactly, but feeling everything just as it had been during those last days.

He had another secret, too, another way of knowing. It was somehow so personal and private that he could never mention it to a soul. He had to keep it shut up inside himself, wrapped in all his senses, bruising and exciting them at the same time; a terrible secret he wished were not his, or, if he must possess it, that he might have just one other person with whom to share it, for it was certainly too much for one little boy to have all by himself. This was a secret telling him so much and yet so little, answering everything but nothing at all.

It had started that night long ago when his mother had screamed. It had waked him and he had climbed out of bed and knocked at the door of their room, calling, "Mama! Mama!" Within the room his mother and father had laughed and told him to go back to bed; everything was all right. But he had not been able to sleep. He had lain awake wondering and listening hard. Only later had he come to understand, had he fitted the pieces of the puzzle together: Red Louis had told The Junior Comanches how he "screwed" the girls in the neighborhood and how one of them, Ruthie Haymes, had once screamed so loud that he had been forced to stop because they were in the hallway of the house where she lived and someone might have heard. Another time Steely and some of his gang had been playing on a roof and had looked down into a room in the back of a lower building. The window had a shade but it had become unhooked, and they could see the man and the woman, naked and sweating like two sleek water animals, locked together, biting, scratching, and rolling, as if they could not let each other go. The other boys had giggled nervously but Steely had crouched as in a trance, his eyes rooted to the feverish, sweat-drenched bodies below. Without wanting to, he had thought of the dogs he and his friends had watched on the street. The comparison had come to his mind instantly and he had wondered at the dirtiness of it all because these two below were not dogs but his own human kind. Horribly fascinated, he had crouched and watched everything, then gone home sick to the stomach, trembling and frightened because he did not know how else to feel.

Then he had come to understand that his mother and father did that too: they lay just that way with their naked bodies. The only thing he could think of was that it was like the dogs on the street. Now he could not help listening for sounds from the other room. And he learned that when they closed the door they did this thing that seemed so nasty to him, and when they left it open they slept as they should, apart from each other, his mother on her side facing the window, his father lying face downward with his head on his arm. Sometimes when they left the door open he would get up late at night and stand long minutes watching them sleep, wondering what determined when they should lie in bed this way or that—and knowing, though he did not want to know, that the strange and violent and naked way was what happened when they were happiest and loved each other and loved the children. He had learned all this by watching their different reactions in the night and the mornings afterward. Steely had gone about obsessed with these thoughts; week after week, month after month, he had given himself to them.

So this was his secret, which seemed so awful to him, his way of knowing they were not happy any more. She said, "Hi, Paul," and he answered, "Hello," and they went into the other room separately, never together as in other times when they used to rush the children to bed before going into the other room together and closing the door. They always left it open now, and Steely could hear nothing but the quiet.

Everything in the house waited; not just his mother and father, but everything: the jet-black gas stove with its two burners, the sink with its cracked porcelain, the fuzzy blue-black flies that sometimes flew through the window and hovered over the pots, Carol Ann's bright yellow painted crib, the two cots on which the boys slept, the big bed in the other room, the green wooden chair. Everything waited as Steely waited, too, knowing that something was to happen, wondering when and what, and knowing that it would be bad.

But when it came, it was in the negative, and so they did not know it had happened until days later. Paul Brown just did not come home, but he might at any moment, and they kept expecting him. Only on the third or fourth day did he know—from the cold hurt look of his mother's eyes and the tight way she held her lips; from this more than anything else—that he should not look for his father from day to day, that Paul had gone away on purpose and would not be back. It struck his mother so deeply she could not cry. It was several months before Steely heard her sobbing in the other room late at night.

In that drowsy state between sleep and consciousness Steely identified the slow, steady creaks of the rusty wheels and was shocked fully awake. He gasped, and stifled his outcry with a tight hand over his own mouth. Black Papa was passing under a street lamp just a few yards away, his white eyes staring straight ahead as if unseeing, his earring catching the light and flinging it back. The mumbled prayer rang softly and clearly in Steely's ears.

Cina, cina, cina,
Dogwé sang, cina lo-gé

The words seemed to pierce Steely's brain and run around and around there. The old man and his cart passed on into the darkness, his prayer just a murmur now in the balmy night. Steely had not moved since he had raised his head. In his fear his imagination ran wild. Surely it was some kind of omen that he had seen Black Papa twice in one night. The old man was a shadow over all the boy's feelings of love and hope and want, of being alone. In the boy's mind he became the dark symbol of all that had happened: the wrong things he had tried to do and must yet do before the night was over; the terrible secret he had held inside so long; the lost money and the lost father.

Steely got up from the bench and walked away. He did not run this time. He was condemned and afraid, but still determined.

nine

Steely walked away from the park at One Hundred and Tenth Street and continued northward on Eighth Avenue. In this early morning hour the rust-red brick buildings drooped their tired dirt-stained jowls of cream-colored window shades as if bored by the monotonous procession of day and night, day and night.

Twice, at different places, Steely passed men who lay on the sidewalk near the curb, but he did not attempt to roll either of them. He could tell, almost from the attitudes of their bodies, that they were derelicts, completely life-wrecked men who had never possessed anything of value. Steely had seen such men all his life and had always been afraid of them, for they were filthy, their smell was nauseating, and their rags of clothing were caked with dirt. They slept troubled but deeply, and seldom bothered to bestir themselves even when their wrecked bodies needed relief. Steely's reaction was one of deep revulsion. He always tried to imagine what their wasted lives had been like but he never could.

In one doorway Steely saw a woman. She was slumped over with her arms around two large shopping bags. She was an old, mustard-colored woman, squat and huge, yet ravaged by time and poor health. All of her features were grotesque, twice as large as they should be, except her eyes, which, closed now, seemed lost in wrinkles of wasted flesh. Her head leaned against the doorway and her toothless mouth gaped open. As Steely hurried past he heard her gruff, sputtering snores and saw the way the wasted flesh of her thick legs seemed to roll down over her shoes. He knew there were men who did not have any money or a place to live, but somehow he had never realized it could happen to a woman. Immediately he thought of his mother and vowed that he would take care of her all his life and never let her grow old and ugly and sick like this gross woman with her great wrinkled arms around the shopping bags.

"Come 'ere, boy!"

Steely jumped. He had not seen the scout car at the curb. Its lights were out and the men within were hardly visible.

"I said come 'ere."

Steely stepped forward hesitantly. He had half a mind to run but was too afraid. He reminded himself that he had not done anything they would know about, but this did not help much. The cop who had spoken was a colored man with a lined brown face in which were set cheerless eyes, glinting coldly in the dim light. The other cop was white, and Steely could not see his face. Steely heard laughter from the far corner and guessed that the two men were spying on the group of people there.

"What's your name, boy?" asked the colored policeman.

"Steely."

"Steely what?"

"Steely Brown."

"Do you know what time it is, Steely Brown?"

"No, sir."

"It's damned near two o'clock in the morning. Did you know that?"

"No, sir."

"Where do you live?"

"A Hundred and Sixteenth Street."

"Well, listen, Steely—that's your name, right?"

Steely nodded.

"Do you want to go to jail?"

Steely shook his head from side to side.

"Well, if you don't want to go to jail . . ." He was looking hard at Steely now and growling in a low voice. ". . . you'd better take some advice I'm gonna give you. I want you to take your little ass and make a beeline for a Hundred and Sixteenth. And if I *ever* catch you out this time of night again, I'm gonna put your little behind in jail and keep you there until you're ninety years old. Do you hear me?" Steely nodded again. "Now beat it, goddamn it, beat it!"

Steely ran toward One Hundred and Sixteenth Street. He wanted to look back but he didn't dare. Remembering the cold eyes, he could almost believe every threatening word. When he had turned down One Hundred and Sixteenth Street and run the whole block to Seventh Avenue, when he was certain the scout car was not following, he turned northward and continued in the direction he had been going.

Now the bars were closing. Some of the emerging men and women laughed and joked on the corners or hurriedly hailed taxis. There were loud, threatening arguments, occasionally resulting in drunken brawls. Steely Brown walked on, turning into first one side street and then another. He knew he must get his mother's twenty-seven dollars at this hour or not at all. He was afraid and excited. The test had come.

The man sat in the doorway with his knees drawn up in front of him. The weight of his body was on one shoulder, pushed against the wall, so the figure seemed like that of a man who had collapsed as he was trying to sit down. The house was set in the darkest part of the street, on one side of which construction was under way, so there was no one to observe Steely from that side. Even though he had been searching he had almost not seen this man, so much a part of the shadows did he seem.

Steely walked by several times to make certain the man was really drunk. Once he walked all the way to the corner to avoid arousing the suspicions of some people who came out of a nearby house. Finally he thought it safe to approach the man, whose position had not changed since Steely had first spotted him.

The wallet was probably in the back pocket of the trousers. Steely would have to lift the tail of the man's jacket, put his hand into the back pocket, and lift out the wallet. It would be almost impossible to perform this operation from the front. Besides, it would be dangerous, for although it was dark, he might be caught in the act by a passer-by. The obvious answer was to step past the man into the vestibule so he could work from behind.

But this Steely hesitated to do. If he had guessed wrong, if the man were not as drunk as Steely hoped, and if he woke up and discovered himself being robbed, Steely would be trapped and unable to run. If luck were against him he would certainly have a better chance to break away if he worked from the front; there would be no chance at all working from behind, for the vestibule would become a narrow prison. He had a vivid picture of the scene: a little boy desperately trying to break out, and a grown man, suddenly awake and angry, blocking the only exit.

But his indecision was short-lived. He *had* to get twenty-seven dollars; and just as he knew he must get it now, so did he know he must get it from this collapsed drunk in the doorway. He would not again be able to summon the strength of purpose, or again submit his mind and body to the same excruciating tension. So he killed all his fear, drowned it in the intense passion eating at him, and gave himself up to this passion—and stepped past the man into the vestibule.

He knelt on one knee and then the other. He paused before lifting the coattail. The back of his intended victim appeared before him as a rounded mass in the general darkness. The man's breath came noisily, as if air were a solid thing that grated on his lungs. Steely put his weight on his knees and one of his hands. With his other he reached forward, slowly, fearing yet anxiously anticipating the thrill of that first second when his fingers would actually touch the fabric of the man's coat. This happened sooner than he expected and he almost jerked his hand away. But he willed down the impulse and kept his fingers resting lightly on the man's back so that the body would become accustomed to his touch. All this he knew to do instinctively, as if the very daring of the act had matured and sharpened his untrained senses. Now his fingers moved quickly as he fought down a panic warning him that every next moment the man would jump up and strike out at him.

The wallet was there! It was in the back pocket where he had hoped it would be, but it was wedged between the buttock and the doorstep where the man slept. He withdrew his hand. He knew what he would have to do: lift the coat, unbutton the pocket, and ease the wallet out as slowly as he could. Any sudden pull at it would be disastrous.

Steely wanted a moment to take a slow deep breath and prepare himself. It seemed as though he had already been in the vestibule for hours. This sense of time pressed in on him, and he could not afford the luxury of the pause he wanted. Taking hold of the coattail, he began to pull slowly and steadily. It was caught between the body and the floor; he knew that, but he must not release it, lest the change wake the sleeping drunk. He continued the pulling pressure, and after a long and terrible moment he felt the coattail begin to move. Slowly . . . slowly . . . little by little . . . it moved.

"Ummm . . ."

The man mumbled and changed his position suddenly. He twisted around so he could sit across the doorway. He lifted his head and let it fall back against the doorsill.

At the first suggestion of movement, Steely had jumped swiftly to his feet and pressed back into the vestibule, quite frozen with sudden terror.

At that moment an automobile passed in the street below and its light illuminated the face of the drunkard. Steely gasped and cried out.

It was the face of his father.

The drunk was Paul Brown.

ten

In that first moment of recognition he had been unable to stop himself from crying out. Then the car passed and the vestibule was dark again.

Everything swirled before him. His breath had rushed out of him as if he had been struck in the stomach. The shock weakened and paralyzed him.

"Pop! Pop!"

His high, piercing voice did not get through to Paul Brown. Steely knelt and took hold of his father's shoulders. He tried to shake Paul, who fell over into the vestibule with a groan. He lay there sprawled in the cubicle, his arms and legs twisted unnaturally like a great broken doll. His lips were parted, showing the teeth white and prominent. This gave his face an exaggerated, almost comic expression, fixing it in a broad, stupid smile. His breathing was regular and noisy, quite undisturbed by Steely's frantic efforts.

"Pop! Pop!" he screamed. "Paul! Paul Brown!"

The shock and the sudden effort had exhausted Steely. He paused to rest, staring at Paul's blurred face. He saw a drunken buffoon.

Steely was suddenly furious. How could *he,* Paul Brown, lie there like that, drunken and dirty, smelling like any bum in the street? How could anybody who had spoken such beautiful words and inspired such challenging dreams—how could he debase himself and lie in such stupor? The contradiction maddened Steely. He slapped out at the ugliness of the face, landing full on the cheek with the palm of his hand. This blow spent, the others followed without his being able to stop them. *Slap! Slap!* Here were Shotgun and the Council who had taken his money, the boys who had beaten him up and taken the bicycle, the purse with only two dollars in it, the betrayals over and over again; everybody and everything that created unhappiness was all here, and he placed his blows one after the other, his open palm stinging and hurting from the blunt contact with skin and bone. *Slap! Slap!* He wanted to keep striking forever, but then he was exhausted again. He fell over into a corner as the hot breath screamed through his empty lungs.

Paul Brown groaned and moved. He put his hands behind him and pushed himself up to a sitting position. His head hung on his chest and his eyes were closed. Once again he groaned, following it with a deep yawn. He began laboriously to move his head from one side to the other as if he were trying to shake it. Feebly he lifted both hands and buried his face in them. He exhaled loudly and groaned again. Now he uncovered his face and really shook his head. He blinked his eyes open and stared dully into the void. He was conscious.

"It's me, Pop. It's Steely."

Paul painfully turned his head and looked toward the sound.

"It's me, Pop." The boy moved closer. "It's Steely."

"Steely? That you, Fred?"

"That's right, Pop. It's me."

"Really you?"

"Really me."

Paul reached into the darkness and put a heavy hand on the boy's head. He touched the familiar features with the tips of his fingers. Then he made an absurd, crying noise in his throat.

"It's you, Fred," as if he had only just discovered it. After a moment he said, "Is this a Hundred and Twenty-ninth Street, Fred?"

"That's right, Pop."

"See what address this is."

Steely had to strain his eyes to see the numbers. He told his father what they were.

"Well, I got to the right house, anyway." His voice was strangely weak. "This is where I live, Fred. Will you help your old man upstairs?"

"Sure, Pop."

With his arm over Steely's shoulders, Paul got to his feet. Steely took a key from his father's pocket and unlocked the door. Together they went up the stairs.

The room was a very small one on the fourth floor. The cot was spread with an army blanket. A reinforced crate in one corner held a small radio. Near the sink was an electric hot plate. There was no window in the room and it was stuffy with a heavy, musty smell.

Paul had gone to the bathroom on the floor below. Steely sat on the cot waiting for him. He was calmer now, almost peaceful. The room and everything it contained seemed familiar to him; he felt as if he had left home with the intention of coming to this very spot. Every possible path had led him here. He had known his father existed, had believed in him and searched for him, and now Steely had found him.

When Paul returned to the room he looked almost refreshed. His tan skin had lost its drunken pallor. He didn't speak to Steely right away. He plugged in the hot plate and set a small white coffeepot on the burner. Then he sat beside his son on the cot and stared at the wall. His gaze was so intent that Steely, who had so much to say, said nothing at all. Thus they sat in silence, one looking at the other, who looked at the wall, as if there were no medium of communication between them. When the coffee in the pot had come to a boil, Paul poured himself a black cupful. Then he half filled another cup, lightened it with milk, and gave it to

Steely. Paul drank his coffee in two long gulps. Finally he said in a shaky voice, "How are Robby and Carol Ann?"

"They're all right," Steely mumbled.

"And your mother? How is she?"

"She's all right, too, I guess."

"And school? How're you doing in school?"

"School's out," the boy said bluntly.

"Oh," said Paul.

He closed his eyes and turned his head toward the wall again. Steely saw that his father's hands were trembling.

Paul was suddenly exasperated with himself. The words seemed to burst out of him. "I don't know what to say to you! I'm sorry, Steely. That's all I can say and I know that's not enough."

He held up his hands and stared at them. "Look at the way they shake. Look at that!"

Steely was puzzled. He had never heard his father talk this way. He scarcely recognized the thin, high-strung voice.

Suddenly Paul looked at Steely. "What the hell were you doing downstairs?" he demanded. "What time is it?" He looked at his watch. "Well, I'll be damned. What the hell are you doing out at this hour?" Now it was the boy who looked away. "Come on. Tell me."

Steely hesitated. He did not expect a grown person to understand how circumstances sometimes forced you to do things you did not want to do. Hadn't his mother said not to come back if he lost the money? And was it his fault that the big boys had robbed him? He had offered to work and work hard, but nobody would advance him the twenty-seven dollars. His father had once told him you had to guard every minute of your life if you expected to become great; that you could make one little wrong turn and never get back on the right road. Well, how could Steely expect him to understand that sometimes you did a wrong in spite of yourself?

But he told Paul anyway, starting at the very beginning and describing everything that had happened. He did this because all these months, he now realized, he had been feeling alone and had carried so much wrapped up inside himself, and now he wanted to reach out and know Paul again. If Paul could not help, who could?

His words tumbled out in a long stream. When he had finished, Paul Brown put a hand on his shoulder and said, "Steely, if I ever hear of you robbing and stealing—well, you see this?" He held his fist in front of Steely's face. It was a real threat, but a smile followed it and Steely felt everything would be all right after all.

Paul stood up. "Now, let's see," he muttered as he looked around the room. "You've got two dollars and change, which means there are twenty-five more standing between you and the worst whipping you ever heard of." He went to the place on the wall where his clothes hung. He took down an overcoat and a suit.

"There's a fellow down in the basement," he said, "a wonderful individual who makes his living out of other people's miseries."

Steely's heart beat faster to hear his father talk in this fashion, which was the way he remembered.

"As much as we detest such individuals, we must perforce deal with them. These clothes and my watch being worth more than a hundred dollars, he may consent to hold them for a fourth of that amount. What do you think?"

It was like a game that had been interrupted for several months, a wonderful game of word magic. Steely nodded his head eagerly.

Paul was gone only a short while. When he came

back he counted out twenty-five dollars, which he pinned to the inside of Steely's pocket. He sat down on the cot and they were silent again.

A new fear came over Steely. If Paul had given him the money, it meant that he had no intention of returning home with Steely. The boy had thought, had dreamed, had known, that when he found Paul they would go home together. Now the question asserted itself in Steely's mind with an urgency that had been growing for several months.

"Pop, can I ask you something?"

"Sure, Steely."

"You gave in, didn't you? Remember how you said that under pressure we shouldn't ever? But you did. You gave in, Pop, didn't you?"

The repetitive accusation brought a sudden flush of guilt to Paul's face. At first it seemed he would not answer, that he could not; and Steely, sensing the effect of his words, wanted to snatch them back and fill the quiet with soft words that would erase the look on his father's face. But he had not yet learned the language of compromise, of live and let live, of give a little and take a little.

Paul said, "Steely, I've got to talk to you and say things I've never said to you before. And I want you to really listen so you'll understand everything." He shifted his position so they faced each other, their eyes meeting directly. "You remember what I told you about Toussaint and Fred Douglas and all those great black men who lived before you and I were born? Well, you've got to believe in them, Steely, and try your best to make your mark the way they did. You've got to believe in them . . . even if you stop believing in me." Here he paused again and swallowed hard. "Because, you see, you're right. I did give in . . . under pressure, I gave in. I just folded up because I wasn't strong enough. I know you thought I was, and so did I, but I wasn't."

He paused and his eyes took on an excited look. "I discovered something I'd never really thought about before: the biggest job is holding onto your sanity. Sure, life is hard, but the greatest danger is within yourself: the thing or combination of things you carry with you that won't let you triumph."

Paul turned away from his son's wide gaze and went on talking, mumbling now, as if he were alone and were explaining things to himself.

"The worst thing in the world is to come face to face with your own mediocrity . . . to know for certain you possess in abundance all the petty weaknesses and appetites you hate . . . to know you don't have the capacity to measure up to the challenge of your own little dream." He jerked his head around and looked at Steely. "Don't you see, all those things I said, I believe. I couldn't measure up, that's all. So you've got to forget about me. Believe in yourself and the dawning greatness of your people, but forget about me."

Steely's eyes smoldered in their deepness. It was Mr. Litchstein . . . Sugar Boy . . . the queer . . . his father. He heard his mother's voice: "Paul Brown, if words was money you'd be a millionaire." Words . . . words . . . Paul Brown was worse than Mr. Litchstein . . . but the boy loved his father . . .

"Go home now, Steely." Paul put his hand on his son's shoulder. Steely twisted away and stood up. He felt the rage of wild fury. Paul said, "I know how you must feel, Steely, but I can't go back with you. I thought you were a big boy and old enough to understand, but maybe you can't."

People . . . they were always betraying you . . . they said one thing and did the other . . . he hated them.

"You're a goddamn liar!" Steely yelled, the words running out of him just as he had heard them on the street. "You're a dirty goddamn liar!"

Paul slapped Steely hard, but the screaming boy didn't feel it.

"Liars! Just liars! Goddamn liars! I don't believe anything you say, and I don't care if you come back or not, and Mama's right when she says you're no goddamn good, and if it wasn't for you, Carol Ann would have enough to eat and so would Robby, and Mama wouldn't have to cry every night if it wasn't for you. I hate you and I hate every god-damn body!"

Suddenly he was crying. For the first time in a long while he did not try to keep the tears from coming. He sobbed and moaned as if he were in pain. When Paul Brown put his arms around him he fought feebly and finally sought shelter in the huge embrace. He had never felt so weak and un-happy in all his life.

"Please come home, Pop," he heard himself say-ing. "Please, Pop, please. Mama's mad at you but she'll let you come back. And everybody wants you back. You have to keep trying, Pop . . . you have to give more than you've got. That's what you said, Pop. Remember?"

Paul Brown hugged Steely very tightly so the boy wouldn't see his face. He closed his eyes. He wanted to go back, but how could he face Mae Brown now? He knew, too, that he had given Steely only words. The boy was too young to know the terrible wrong he had done. The boy could never understand the thousand little enemies a man carried within himself that had pulled Paul away from home. Perhaps, if he really tried, he could make the boy believe something high-sounding and noble. But he couldn't fool himself and he couldn't fool Mae Brown. He could hurt her but he couldn't make her believe in what wasn't there. How could he go back?

Yet he was imprisoned by the boy's sensitive love and faith. His mind played with a biblical phrase: *Man* created *God* in his own image. And all the black heroes he had created for the boy were dead and gone to hell if they did not live in Paul Brown.

Later they emerged from the house and walked toward One Hundred and Sixteenth Street. Already the dark of night was passing and the morning winds whipped briskly through the Harlem streets. Paul had bathed and changed his clothes and, in Steely's opinion, had never looked so good. Steely skipped once so that he could walk in step with his father.

When they stopped at a corner the man spoke with mock severity. "You think you're pretty smart, don't you?

"*Oh, boy*," said Steely, flashing one of his rare smiles as he threw Paul's favorite expression back at him.

Arm in arm they walked through Harlem in the morning. That's the best time of all, morning, because then the air is fresh and clean, and, although the people sleep, there is the sense of awakening.